13 CHILLING GHOST STORIES

SELECTED BY
RUSKIN BOND

Published by Westland Books, a division of Nasadiya Technologies Private Limited, in 2024

No. 269/2B, First Floor, 'Irai Arul', Vimalraj Street, Nethaji Nagar, Alapakkam Main Road, Maduravoyal, Chennai 600095

Westland and the Westland logo are the trademarks of Nasadiya Technologies Private Limited, or its affiliates.

Anthology copyright © Nasadiya Technologies Pvt Ltd, 2024

This is a work of fiction. Names, characters, organisations, places, events and incidents are either products of the authors' imagination or used fictitiously.

ISBN: 9789360454210
10 9 8 7 6 5 4 3 2 1

Printed at Nutech Print Services, India

Contents

From the Editor's Desk

Over the years, my fascination with the supernatural has led me to explore countless tales of hauntings and spectral encounters.

I have written several stories with ghosts playing the lead role. And before I go any further, I must tell you the story of the ghost that haunted a famous playback singer's house in Mumbai. I heard it from Vidhi, my editor, who spent many years in Mumbai, where she knew many film people.

Ms B, as most of us will know, is a great singer, whose voice has been part of soundtracks of hundreds of films.

Many decades ago, she was looking for a bungalow in a quiet part of Mumbai and took a fancy to an old mansion because it had 'character'. Someone had told her it was haunted but the singer wasn't afraid of ghosts; living beings are usually more dangerous.

Anyway, she bought the place and moved in. Before long, she had created a beautiful home, admired by all.

Then one night, as she was about to retire to her bedroom, the ghost appeared—a good-looking gentleman in an old-fashioned costume, obviously a spectator from the distant past.

'Will you sing for me?' he asked politely.

Ms B, who is a good sport with a great sense of humour, decided to humour the ghost and crooned a rendition of one of her most popular songs.

The ghost looked pleased, thanked her humbly and vanished into the night.

A few days later, he appeared again and asked for another song. Ms B obliged. He offered her his thanks and departed.

These encounters took place from time to time until, late one evening when the lights were low and the sea was a distant symphony, Ms B countered the ghost's request with a question: 'And who are you, dear sir? You are obviously the spirit of a music lover.'

'I'm the ghost of Tansen,' replied the spirit. 'And I would be honoured if you were to sing a duet with me.'

Tansen, you see, was the great singer who performed at the court of Emperor Akbar, some four hundred years earlier. Ms B graciously agreed to sing with him.

Their voices blended beautifully. It was summer and the windows were open; the song was carried with the wind and could be heard all over the city. The good people of Mumbai slept peacefully that night. The song could be heard everywhere—a song of dreams and roses and nightingales.

But it was the last appearance of the ghost.

Entire Mumbai is waiting for it to return, so that they can enjoy another wonderful concert by two great artists, one from the past and one from the present.

Carrying on the tradition of reading and writing tales about ghosts and ghouls, welcome to another journey into the eerie and enthralling world of ghost stories.

Ghost stories are one of the oldest of all the supernatural literary genres that have captured the imagination of almost every writer including me. And, I am delighted to present to you this carefully curated anthology of 13 all-time best ghost stories, chosen for their timeless appeal and chilling narratives.

It is my love for the eerie and paranormal that inspired me to curate this collection of ghost stories. I have tried to follow my keen sense of the supernatural to collect the most chilling and uncanny tales in the canon. This selection brings together evergreen classic ghost stories that have stood the test of time while still captivating readers with their bone-chilling charm.

This anthology is created with the desire to explore several themes often featured in ghost stories—the unknown, the unresolved and the uncanny. These themes are not only entertaining but also provoke deep reflections on life, death and that which lies beyond it.

The selection of these stories is based on the unique ways they engage with the supernatural, their historical importance and cultural influence.

Ghost stories have been part of human narratives since time immemorial; they help explain unexplainable things while they entertain readers. This anthology is a representation of this rich history that incorporates diverse cultural references alongside folklore that have shaped this genre.

Among the stories, you will find works by noteworthy authors like Nathaniel Hawthorne, H.P. Lovecraft and Edith Nesbit. These authors have made a significant and unique contribution, to the genre, with their own style. This enriches this collection with diverse voices and haunting experiences.

I must acknowledge the creativity and efforts of all the contributing authors. Their ability to pen such compelling narratives is truly commendable. It is their stories that make this anthology a treasure trove of ghostly encounters.

As you immerse yourself in these stories, I encourage you to let your imagination roam free. Allow yourself to be drawn into the mysterious and the macabre, and perhaps even question what you believe about the supernatural.

I hope that your imagination runs wild as you delve into these stories. Let yourself be pulled through the mysterious and the macabre and question, even for a moment, what you believe in the supernatural. These stories of the strange and supernatural will fascinate you and haunt you, as they have haunted millions of readers before you, as they add to the rich tapestry of ghost lore.

Enjoy reading. May the *spirits* be with you!

Ruskin Bond
Mussoorie, India
September 2024.

The Ghost of Dr Harris

Nathaniel Hawthorne

I am afraid this ghost story will be a very faded aspect when transferred to paper. Whatever effect it had on you, or whatever charm it retains in your memory, is perhaps to be attributed to the favourable circumstances under which it was originally told.

We were sitting, I remember, late in the evening, in your drawing room, where the lights of the chandelier were so muffled as to produce a delicious obscurity through which the fire diffused a dim red glow. In this rich twilight, the feelings of the party had been properly attuned by some tales of English superstition, and the lady of Smithills Hall had just been describing that Bloody Footstep which marks the threshold of her old mansion when your Yankee guest (zealous for the honour of his country, and desirous of proving that his dead compatriots have the same ghostly privileges as other dead people, if they think it worthwhile to use them) began a story of something wonderful that long ago happened to himself. Possibly in the verbal narrative he may have assumed a little more license than would be allowable in a written record. For the sake of the artistic effect, he may then have thrown in, here and there, a few slight circumstances which he will not think it proper to retain in what he now puts forth as the sober statement of a veritable fact.

A good many years ago (it must be as many as fifteen, perhaps more, and while I was still a bachelor) I resided in Boston, in the United States. In that city there is a large and long-established library, styled the Athenaeum, connected with which is a reading room, well supplied with foreign and American periodicals and newspapers. A splendid edifice has since been erected by the proprietors of the institution; but, at the period I speak of, it was contained within a large old mansion, formerly the town residence of an eminent citizen of Boston. The reading room (a spacious hall, with the group of the Laocoon at one end, and the Belvedere Apollo at the other) was frequented by not a few elderly merchants, retired from business, by clergymen and lawyers, and by such literary men as we had amongst us. These good people were mostly old, leisurely and somnolent, and used to nod and doze for hours together with the newspapers before them. And then recovering themselves as far as to read a word or two of the politics of the day sitting, as, as it were, on the boundary of the Land of Dreams, and having little to do with this world, except through the newspapers which they so tenaciously grasped.

One of these worthies, whom I occasionally saw there, was the Reverend Doctor Harris, a Unitarian clergyman of considerable repute and eminence. He was very far advanced in life, not less than eighty years old, and probably more; and he resided, I think, at Dorchester, a suburban village near Boston. I had never been personally acquainted with this good old clergyman, but had heard of him all my life as a noteworthy man; so that when he was first pointed out to me, I looked at him with a certain speciality of attention, and always subsequently eyed him with a degree of interest whenever I happened to see him at the Athenaeum or elsewhere. He was a small, withered, infirm, but brisk old gentleman, with snow-white hair, a somewhat stooping figure, but yet a remarkable alacrity of movement. I remember it was in the street that I first noticed him. The Doctor was plodding along with a staff, but turned smartly about on being addressed by the gentleman who was with me, and responded with a good deal of vivacity.

'Who is he?' I inquired, as soon as he had passed. 'The Reverend Doctor Harris, of Dorchester', replied

my companion; and from that time, I often saw him, and never forgot his aspect. His special haunt was the Athenaeum. There I used to see him daily, and almost always with a newspaper the *Boston Post*, which was the leading journal of the Democratic Party in the Northern States. As old doctor Harris had been a noted Democrat during his more active life, it was a very natural thing, it was a very natural thing that he should still like to read the *Boston Post*. There his reverend figure was accustomed to sit day after day, in the self-same chair by the fireside; and, by degrees, seeing him there so constantly, I began to look towards him as I entered the reading room, and felt that a kind of acquaintance, at least on my part, was established. Not that I had any reason (as long as this venerable person remained in the body) to suppose that he ever noticed me; but by some subtle connection, that small, white-haired, infirm, yet vivacious figure of an old clergyman became associated with my idea and recollection of the place. One day especially (about noon, as was generally his hour) I am perfectly certain that I had seen this figure of old Doctor Harris, and taken my customary note of him, although I remember nothing in his appearance at all different from what I had seen on many previous occasions.

But, that very evening, a friend said to me: 'Did you hear that old Doctor Harris is dead?' 'No,' said I very quietly, 'it cannot be true; for I saw him at the Athenaeum today.' 'You must be mistaken,' rejoined my friend. 'He is certainly dead!' and confirmed the fact with such special circumstances that I could no longer doubt it. My friend has often since assured me that I seemed much startled as the intelligence; but, as well as I can recollect, I believe that I was very little disturbed, if at all, but set down the apparition as a mistake of my own, or, perhaps, the interposition of a familiar idea into the place and amid the circumstances with which I had been accustomed to associate it.

The next day, as I ascended the steps of the Athenaeum, I remember thinking within myself: 'Well, I never shall see old Doctor Harris again!' With this thought in my mind, as I opened the door of the reading room, I glanced towards the spot and chair where Doctor Harris usually sat, and there, to my astonishment, sat the grey, infirm figure of the deceased Doctor, reading the newspaper as was his wont! His own death must have been recorded, that very morning, in that very newspaper! I have no recollection of being greatly discomposed at the moment, or indeed that I felt any extraordinary emotion whatever. Probably, if ghosts were in the habit of coming among us, they would coincide with the ordinary train of affairs, and melt into them so familiarly that we should not be shocked at their presence. At all events, so it was in this instance. I looked through the newspapers as usual, and turned over the periodicals, taking about as much interest in their contents as at other times. Once or twice, no doubt, I may have lifted my eyes from the page to look again at the venerable Doctor, who ought then to have been lying in his coffin dressed out for the grave, but who felt such interest in the *Boston Post* as to come back from the other world to read it the morning after his death. One might have supposed that he would have cared more about the novelties of the sphere to which he had just been introduced than about the politics he had left behind him! The apparition took no notice of me, nor behaved otherwise in any respect than on any previous day. Nobody but myself seemed to notice him, and yet the old gentlemen round about the fire, beside his chair, were his lifelong acquaintances, who were perhaps thinking of his death, and who in a day or two would deem it a proper courtesy to attend his funeral.

I have forgotten how the ghost of Doctor Harris took its departure from the Athenaeum on this occasion, or, in fact, whether the ghost or I went first. This equanimity, and almost indifference, on my part the careless way in which I glanced at so singular a mystery and left it aside is what now surprises me as much as anything else in the affair.

From that time, for a long time there after for weeks at least, and I know not but for months I used to see the figure of Doctor Harris quite as frequently as before his death. It grew to be so common that at length I regarded the venerable defunct no more than any other of the old fogies who basked before the fire and dozed over the newspapers.

It was but a ghost nothing but thin air not tangible nor appreciable, nor demanding any attention from a man of flesh and blood! I cannot recollect any cold shudderings, any awe, any repugnance, any emotion whatever, such as would be suitable and decorous on beholding a visitant from the spiritual world. It is very strange, but such is the truth. It appears excessively odd to me now that I did not adopt such means as I readily might to ascertain whether the appearance had solid substance, or was merely gaseous and vapoury. I might have brushed against him, jostled his chair or accidentally trodden on his poor old toes. I might have snatched the *Boston Post* unless that were an apparition too, out of his shadowy hands. I might have tested him in a hundred ways; but I did nothing of the kind.

Perhaps I was loath to destroy the illusion, and to rob myself of so good a ghost story, which might probably have been explained in some very commonplace way. Perhaps, after all, I had a secret dread of the old phenomenon, and therefore kept within my limits, with an instinctive caution which I mistook for indifference. Be this as it may, here is the fact. I saw the figure, day after day, for a considerable space of time, and took no pains to ascertain whether it was a ghost or no. I never, to my knowledge, saw him come into the reading room or depart from it. There sat Doctor Harris in his customary chair, and I can say little else about him.

After a certain period, I really know not how long I began to notice, or to fancy, a peculiar regard in the old gentleman's aspect towards myself. I sometimes found him gazing at me, and, unless I deceived myself, there was a sort of expectancy in his face. His spectacles, I think, were shoved up, so that his bleared eyes might meet my own. Had he been a living man I should have flattered myself that good Doctor Harris was, for some reason or other, interested in me and desirous of a personal acquaintance. Being a ghost, and amenable to ghostly laws, it was natural to conclude that he was waiting to be spoken to before delivering whatever message he wished to impart. But, if so, the ghost had shown the bad judgement common among the spiritual brotherhood, both as regarded the place of interview and the person whom he had selected as the recipient of his communications. In the reading room of the Athenaeum conversation is strictly forbidden, and I could not have addressed the apparition without drawing the instant notice and indignant frowns of the slumberous old gentlemen around me. I myself, too, at that time, was shy as any ghost, and followed the ghosts' rule never to speak first. And what an absurd figure should I have made, solemnly and awfully addressing what must have appeared, in the eyes of all the rest of the company, an empty chair! Besides, I had never been introduced to Doctor Harris, dead or alive, and I am not aware that social regulations are to be abrogated by the accidental fact of one of the parties having crossed the imperceptible line which separates the other party from the spiritual world. If ghosts throw off all conventionalism among themselves, it does not therefore follow that it can be safely dispensed with by those who are still hampered with flesh and blood.

For such reasons as these, that the deceased Doctor might burden me with some disagreeable tasks, with which I had no business nor wish to be concerned, I stubbornly resolved to have nothing to say to him. To this determination I adhered. Not a syllable ever passed between the ghost of Doctor Harris and myself.

To the best of my recollection, I never observed the old gentleman either enter the reading room or depart from it, move from his chair or lay down the newspaper, or exchange a look with any person in the company, unless it were myself. He was not by any means invariably in his place. In the evening, for instance, though often at the reading room myself, I never saw him. It was at the brightest noon time that I used to behold him, sitting within the most comfortable focus of the glowing fire, as real and lifelike an object (except that he was so very old, and of an ashen complexion) as any other in the room. After a long while of this strange intercourse, if such it can be called, I remember once at least, and I know not but oftener a sad, wistful, disappointed gaze, which the ghost fixed upon me from beneath his spectacles; a melancholy look of helplessness, which, if my heart had not been as hard as a paving-stone, I could hardly have withstood. But I did withstand it; and I think I saw him no more after this last appealing look, which still dwells in my memory as perfectly as while my own eyes were encountering the dim and bleared eyes of the ghost. And whenever I recall this strange passage of my life, I see the small, old withered figure of Dr Harris, sitting in his accustomed chair, the *Boston Post* in his hand, his spectacles shoved upwards and gazing at me as I close the door of the reading room, with that wistful, appealing, hopeless, helpless look. It is too late now: his grave has been grass-grown this many and many a year; and I hope he has found rest in it without any aid from me.

I have only to add that it was not until long after I had ceased to encounter the ghost that I became aware how very odd and strange the whole affair had been; and even now I am made sensible of its strangeness chiefly by the wonder and incredulity of those to whom I tell the story.

2

The Terrible Old Man

H.P. Lovecraft

It was the design of Angelo Ricci, Joe Czanek and Manuel Silva to call on the Terrible Old Man. This old man dwells all alone in a very ancient house on Water Street near the sea, and is reputed to be both exceedingly rich and exceedingly feeble; which forms a situation very attractive to men of the profession of Messrs. Ricci, Czanek, and Silva, for that profession was nothing less dignified than robbery.

The inhabitants of Kingsport say and think many things about the Terrible Old Man which generally keep him safe from the attention of gentlemen like Mr Ricci and his colleagues, despite the almost certain fact that he hides a fortune of indefinite magnitude somewhere about his musty and venerable abode. He is, in truth, a very strange person, believed to have been a captain of East India clipper ships in his day; so old that no one can remember when he was young, and so taciturn that few know his real name. Among the gnarled trees in the front yard of his aged and neglected place he maintains a strange collection of large stones, oddly grouped and painted so that they resemble the idols in some obscure Eastern temple. This collection frightens away most of the small boys who love to taunt the Terrible Old Man about his long white hair and beard, or to break the small-paned windows of his dwelling with wicked missiles. But there are other things which frighten the older and more curious folk who sometimes steal up to the house to peer in through the dusty panes. These folk say that on a table in a bare room on the ground floor are many peculiar bottles, in each a small piece of lead suspended pendulum-wise from a string. And they say that the Terrible Old Man talks to these bottles, addressing them by such names as Jack, Scar-Face, Long Tom, Spanish Joe, Peters and Mate Ellis, and that whenever he speaks to a bottle the little lead pendulum within makes certain definite vibrations as if in answer. Those who have watched the tall, lean, Terrible Old Man in these peculiar conversations, do not watch him again. But Angelo Ricci, Joe Czanek and Manuel Silva were not of Kingsport blood; they were of that new and heterogeneous alien stock which lies outside the charmed circle of New England life and traditions, and they saw in the Terrible Old Man merely a tottering, almost helpless greybeard, who could not walk without the aid of his knotted cane, and whose thin, weak hands shook pitifully. They were really quite sorry in their way for the lonely, unpopular old fellow, whom everybody shunned, and at whom all the dogs barked singularly. But business is business, and to a robber whose soul is in his profession, there is a lure and a challenge about a very old and very feeble man who has no account at the bank, and who pays for his few necessities at the village store with Spanish gold and silver minted two centuries ago.

Messrs. Ricci, Czanek and Silva selected the night of 11 April for their call. Mr Ricci and Mr Silva were to interview the poor old gentleman, whilst Mr Czanek waited for them and their presumable metallic burden with a covered motor car in Ship Street, by the gate in the tall rear wall of their host's grounds. Desire to avoid needless explanations in case of unexpected police intrusions, these plans prompted a quiet and unostentatious departure.

As prearranged, the three adventurers started out separately in order to prevent any evil-minded suspicions afterwards. Messrs. Ricci and Silva met in Water Street by the old man's front gate, and although they did not like the way the moon shone down upon the painted stones through the budding branches of the gnarled trees, they had more important things to think about than mere idle superstition. They feared it might be unpleasant work making the Terrible Old Man loquacious concerning his hoarded gold and silver, for aged sea captains are notably stubborn and perverse. Still, he was very old and very feeble, and there were two visitors. Messrs. Ricci and Silva were experienced in the art of making unwilling persons voluble, and the screams of a weak and exceptionally venerable man can be easily muffled. So, they moved up to the one-lighted window and heard the Terrible Old Man talking childishly to his bottles with pendulums. Then they donned masks and knocked politely at the weather-stained oaken door.

Waiting seemed very long to Mr Czanek as he fidgeted restlessly in the covered motor car by the Terrible Old Man's back gate in Ship Street. He was more than ordinarily tender-hearted, and he did not like the hideous screams he had heard in the ancient house just after the hour appointed for the deed. Had he not told his colleagues to be as gentle as possible with the pathetic old sea captain? Very nervously he watched that narrow oaken gate in the high and ivy-clad stone wall. Frequently he consulted his watch, and wondered at the delay. Had the old man died before

revealing where his treasure was hidden, and had a thorough search become necessary? Mr Czanek did not like to wait so long in the dark in such a place. Then he sensed a soft tread or tapping on the walk inside the gate, heard a gentle fumbling at the rusty latch, and saw the narrow, heavy door swing inward. And in the pallid glow of the single dim street-lamp he strained his eyes to see what his colleagues had brought out of that sinister house which loomed so close behind. But when he looked, he did not see what he had expected; for his colleagues were not there at all, but only the Terrible Old Man leaning quietly on his knotted cane and smiling hideously. Mr Czanek had never before noticed the colour of that man's eyes; now he saw that they were yellow.

Little things make considerable excitement in little towns, which is the reason that Kingsport people talked all that spring and summer about the three unidentifiable bodies, horribly slashed as with many cutlasses, and horribly mangled as by the tread of many cruel boot-heels, which the tide washed in. And some people even spoke of things as trivial as the deserted motor car found on Ship Street, or certain especially inhuman cries, probably of a stray animal or migratory bird, heard in the night by wakeful citizens. But in this idle village gossip the Terrible Old Man took no interest at all. He was by nature reserved, and when one is aged and feeble one's reserve is doubly strong. Besides, so ancient a sea captain must have witnessed scores of things much more stirring in the far-off days of his unremembered youth.

3

The Haunted Dolls' House

M.R. James

'I suppose you get stuff of that kind through your hands pretty often?' said Mr Dillet, as he pointed with his stick to an object which shall be described when the time comes: and when he said it, he lied in his throat and knew that he lied. Not once in twenty years—perhaps not once in a lifetime—could Mr Chittenden, skilled as he was in ferreting out the forgotten treasures of half-a-dozen counties, expect to handle such a specimen. It was collectors' palaver, and Mr Chittenden recognised it as such.

'Stuff of that kind, Mr Dillet! It's a museum piece, that is.'

'Well, I suppose there are museums that'll take anything.'

'I've seen one, not as good as that, years back,' said Mr Chittenden, thoughtfully.

'But that's not likely to come into the market: and I'm told they 'ave some fine ones of the period over the water. No: I'm only telling you the truth, Mr Dillet, when I say that if you was to place an unlimited order with me for the very best that could be got—and you know I 'ave facilities for getting to know of such things, and a reputation to maintain—well, all I can say is, I should lead you straight up to that one and say, "I can't do no better for you than that, Sir."'

'Hear, hear!' said Mr Dillet, applauding ironically with the end of his stick on the floor of the shop. 'How much are you sticking the innocent American buyer for it, eh?'

'Oh, I shan't be over hard on the buyer, American or otherwise. You see, it stands this way, Mr Dillet—if I knew just a bit more about the pedigree—'

'Or just a bit less,' Mr Dillet put in.

'Ha, ha! You will have your joke, Sir. No, but as I was saying, if I knew just a little more than what I do about the piece—though anyone can see for themselves it's a genuine thing, every last corner of it, and there's not been one of my men allowed to so much as touch it since it came into the shop—there'd be another figure in the price I'm asking.'

'And what's that: five and twenty?'

'Multiply that by three and you've got it, Sir. Seventy-five's my price.'

'And fifty's mine,' said Mr Dillet.

The point of agreement was, of course, somewhere between the two, it does not matter exactly where—I think sixty guineas. But half an hour later the object was being packed, and within an hour Mr Dillet had called for it in his car and driven away. Mr Chittenden, holding the cheque in his hand, saw him off from the door with smiles, and returned, still smiling, into the parlour where his wife was making the tea. He stopped at the door.

'It's gone,' he said.

'Thank God for that!' said Mrs Chittenden, putting down the teapot. 'Mr Dillet, was it?'

'Yes, it was.'

'Well, I'd sooner it was him than another.'

'Oh, I don't know, he ain't a bad feller, my dear.'

'Maybe not, but in my opinion he'd be none the worse for a bit of a shake-up.'

'Well, if that's your opinion, it's my opinion he's put himself into the way of getting one. Anyhow, we shan't have any more of it, and that's something to be thankful for.'

And so Mr and Mrs Chittenden sat down to tea.

And what of Mr Dillet and his new acquisition? What it was, the title of this story will have told you. What it was like, I shall have to indicate as well as I can.

There was only just room enough for it in the car, and Mr Dillet had to sit with the driver: he had also to go slow, for though the rooms of the Doll's House had all been stuffed carefully with soft cotton-wool, jolting was to be avoided, in view of the immense number of small objects which thronged them; and the ten-mile drive was an anxious time for him, in spite of all the precautions he insisted upon. At last, his front door was reached, and Collins, the butler, came out.

'Look here, Collins, you must help me with this thing—it's a delicate job. We must get it out upright, see? It's full of little things that mustn't be displaced more than we can help. Let's see, where shall we have it? (After a pause for consideration). Really, I think I shall have to put it in my own room, to begin with at any rate. On the big table—that's it.'

It was conveyed—with much talking—to Mr Dillet's spacious room on the first floor, looking out on the drive. The sheeting was unwound from it, and the front thrown open, and for the next hour or two Mr Dillet was fully occupied in extracting the padding and setting in order the contents of the rooms.

When this thoroughly congenial task was finished, I must say that it would have been difficult to find a more perfect and attractive specimen of a Doll's House in Strawberry Hill Gothic than that which now stood on Mr Dillet's large kneehole table, lighted up by the evening sun which came slanting through three tall sash windows.

It was quite six feet long, including the Chapel or Oratory which flanked the front on the left as you faced it, and the stable on the right. The main block of the house was, as I have said, in the Gothic manner: that is to say, the windows had pointed arches and were surmounted by what are called ogival hoods, with crockets and finials such as we see on the canopies of tombs built into church walls. At the angles were absurd turrets covered with arched panels. The Chapel had pinnacles and buttresses, a bell in the turret and coloured glass in the windows. When the front of the house was open you saw four large rooms, a bedroom, dining room, drawing room and kitchen, each with its appropriate furniture in a very complete state.

The stable on the right was in two storeys, with its proper complement of horses, coaches and grooms, and with its clock and Gothic cupola for the clock bell.

Pages, of course, might be written on the outfit of the mansion—how many frying pans, how many gilt chairs, what pictures, carpets, chandeliers, four-posters, table linen, glass, crockery and plate it possessed; but all this

must be left to the imagination. I will only say that the base or plinth on which the house stood (for it was fitted with one of some depth which allowed a flight of steps to the front door and a terrace, partly balustraded) contained a shallow drawer or drawers in which were neatly stored sets of embroidered curtains, changes of raiment for the inmates, and, in short, all the materials for an infinite series of variations and refittings of the most absorbing and delightful kind.

'Quintessence of Horace Walpole, that's what it is: he must have had something to do with the making of it.' Such was Mr Dillet's murmured reflection as he knelt before it in a reverent ecstasy. 'Simply wonderful! This is my day and no mistake. Five hundred pounds coming in this morning for that cabinet which I never cared about, and now this tumbling into my hands for a tenth, at the very most, of what it would fetch in town. Well, well! It almost makes one afraid something will happen to counter it. Let's have a look at the population, anyhow.'

Accordingly, he set them before him in a row. Again, here is an opportunity, which some would snatch at, of making an inventory of costume: I am incapable of it.

There were a gentleman and lady, in blue satin and brocade respectively. There were two children, a boy and a girl. There was a cook, a nurse, a footman, and there were the stable servants, two postillions, a coachman and two grooms.

'Anyone else? Yes, possibly.'

The curtains of the four-poster in the bedroom were closely drawn around four sides of it, and he put his finger in between them and felt in the bed. He drew the finger back hastily, for it almost seemed to him as if something had—not stirred, perhaps, but yielded—in an odd live way as he pressed it. Then he put back the curtains, which ran on rods in the proper manner, and extracted from the bed a white-haired old gentleman in a long linen night dress and cap, and laid him down by the rest. The tale was complete.

Dinner time was now near, so Mr Dillet spent but five minutes in putting the lady and children into the drawing room, the gentleman into the dining room, the servants into the kitchen and stables, and the old man back into his bed. He retired into his dressing room next door, and we see and hear no more of him until something like eleven o'clock at night.

His whim was to sleep surrounded by some of the gems of his collection. The big room in which we have seen him contained his bed: bath, wardrobe, and all the appliances of dressing were in a commodious room adjoining: but his four-poster, which itself was a valued treasure, stood in the large room where he sometimes wrote, and often sat, and even received visitors. Tonight he repaired to it in a highly complacent frame of mind.

There was no striking clock within earshot— none on the staircase, none in the stable, none in the distant Church tower. Yet it is indubitable that Mr Dillet was startled out of a very pleasant slumber by a bell tolling One.

He was so startled that he did not merely lie breathless with wide-open eyes but sat up in his bed.

He never asked himself, till the morning hours, how it was that, though there was no light at all in the room, the Doll's House on the kneehole table stood out with complete clearness. But it was so. The effect was that of a bright harvest moon shining full on the front of a big white stone mansion—a quarter of a mile away it might be, and yet every detail was photographically sharp. There were trees about it, too—trees rising behind the chapel and the house. He seemed to be conscious of the scent of a cool still September night. He thought he could hear an occasional stamp and clink from the stables, as of horses stirring. And with another shock, he realised that, above the house, he was looking, not at the wall of his room with its pictures, but into the profound blue of a night sky.

There were lights, more than one, in the windows, and he quickly saw that this was no four-roomed house with a movable front, but one of many rooms, and staircases—a real house, but seen as if through the wrong end of a telescope. 'You mean to show me something,' he muttered to himself, and he gazed earnestly at the lighted windows. They would in real life have been shuttered or curtained, no doubt, he thought; but, as it was, there was nothing to intercept his view of what was being transacted inside the rooms.

Two rooms were lighted—one on the ground floor to the right of the door, one upstairs, on the left—the first brightly enough, the other rather dimly. The lower room was the dining room: a table was laid, but the meal was over, and only wine and glasses were left on the table. The man of the blue satin and the woman of the brocade were alone in the room, and they were talking very earnestly, seated close together at the table, their elbows on it. Every now and again stopping to listen, as it seemed. Oncehe rose, came to the window, opened it and put his head out and his hand to his ear. There was a lighted taper in a silver candlestick on a sideboard. When the man left the window he seemed to leave the room also; and the lady, taper in hand, remained standing and listening. The expression on her face was that of one striving her utmost to keep down a fear that threatened to master her—and succeeding. It was a hateful face, too; broad, flat and sly. Now the man came back and she took some small thing from him and hurried out of the room. He, too, disappeared, but only for a moment or two. The front door slowly opened and he stepped out and stood on the top of theperron, looking this way and that; then turned towards the upper window that was lighted, and shook his fist.

It was time to look at that upper window. Through it was seen a four-post bed: a nurse or other servant in an armchair, evidently sound asleep; in the bed an old man lying: awake, and, one would say, anxious, from how he shifted about and moved his fingers, beating tunes on the coverlet. Beyond the bed, a door opened. The light was seen on the ceiling, and the lady came in: she set down her candle on a table, came to the fireside and roused the nurse. In her hand, she had an old-fashioned wine bottle, ready uncorked. The nurse took it, poured some of the contents into a little silver saucepan, added some spice and sugar from casters on the table, and set it to warm on the fire. Meanwhile, the old man in the bed beckoned feebly to the lady, who came to him, smiling, took his wrist as if to feel his pulse, and bit her lip as if in consternation. He looked at her anxiously and then pointed to the window, and spoke. She nodded, and did as the man below had done; opened the casement and listened—perhaps rather ostentatiously: then drew in her head and shook it, looking at the old man, who seemed to sigh.

By this time the posset on the fire was steaming, and the nurse poured it into a small two-handled silver bowl and brought it to the bedside. The old man seemed disinclined for it and was waving it away, but the lady and the nurse together bent over him and evidently pressed it upon him. He must have yielded, for they supported him into a sitting position, and put it to his lips. He drank most of it, in several draughts, and they laid him down. The lady left the room, smiling goodnight to him, and took the bowl, the bottle and the silver saucepan with her. The nurse returned to the chair, and there was an interval of complete quiet.

Suddenly the old man started up in his bed—and he must have uttered some cry, for the nurse started out of her chair and made but one step of it to the bedside. He was a sad and terrible sight—flushed in the face, almost to blackness, the eyes glaring whitely, both hands clutching at his heart, foam at his lips.

For a moment the nurse left him, ran to the door, flung it wide open, and, one supposes, screamed aloud for help, then darted back to the bed and seemed to try feverishly to soothe him—to lay him down—anything. But as the lady, her husband, and several servants, rushed into the room with horrified faces, the old man collapsed under the nurse's hands and lay back, and the features, contorted with agony and rage, relaxed slowly into calm.

A few moments later, lights showed out to the left of the house, and a coach with flambeaux drove up to the door. A white-wigged man in black got nimbly out and ran up the steps, carrying a small leather trunk-shaped box. He was met in the doorway by the man and his wife, she with her handkerchief clutched between her hands, he with a tragic face, but retaining his self-control. They led the newcomer into the dining room, where he set his box of papers on the table, and, turning to them, listened with a face of consternation at what they had to tell. He nodded his head again and again, threw out his hands slightly, declined, it seemed, offers of refreshment and lodging for the night, and within a few minutes came slowly down the steps entering the coach and driving off the way he had come. As the man in blue watched him from the top of the steps, a smile not pleasant to see stole slowly over his fat white face. Darkness fell over the whole scene as the lights of the coach disappeared.

But Mr Dillet remained sitting up in the bed: he had rightly guessed that there would be a sequel. The house front glimmered out again before long. But now there was a difference. The lights were in other windows, one at the top of the house, the other illuminating the range of coloured windows of the chapel. How he saw through these is not quite obvious, but he did. The interior was as carefully furnished as the rest of the establishment, with its minute red cushions on the desks, its Gothic stall canopies, and its western gallery and pinnacled organ with gold pipes. On the centre of the black and white pavement was a bier: four tall candles burned at the corners. On the bier was a coffin covered with a pall of black velvet.

As he looked the folds of the pall stirred. It seemed to rise at one end: it slid downwards: it fell away, exposing the black coffin with its silver handles and nameplate. One of the tall candlesticks swayed and toppled over. Ask no more, but turn, as Mr Dillet hastily did, and look in at the lighted window at the top of the house, where a boy and girl lay in two truckle-beds, and a four-poster for the nurse rose above them. The nurse was not visible for the moment; but the father and mother were there, dressed now in mourning, but with very little sign of mourning in their demeanour. Indeed, they were laughing and talking with a good deal of animation, sometimes to each other, and sometimes throwing a remark to one or other of the children, and again laughing at the answers. Then the father was seen to go on tiptoe out of the room, taking with him as he went a white garment that hung on a peg near the door. He shut the door after him. A minute or two later it was slowly opened again, and a muffled head poked round it. A bent form of sinister shape stepped across to the truckle-beds and suddenly stopped, threw up its arms and revealed, of course, the father, laughing. The children were in agonies of terror, the boy with the bedclothes over his head, the girl throwing herself out of bed into her mother's arms. Attempts at consolation followed—the parents took the children on their laps, patted them, picked up the white gown and showed there was no harm in it, and so forth; and at last putting the children back into bed, left the room with encouraging waves of the hand. As they left it, the nurse came in, and soon the light died down.

Still, Mr Dillet watched immovable.

A new sort of light—not of lamp or candle—a pale ugly light, began to dawn around the door-case at the back of the room. The door was opening again. The seer does not like to dwell upon what he saw entering the room: he says it might be described as a frog—the size of a man—but it had scanty white hair about its head. It was busy about the truckle-beds, but not for long. The sound of cries—faint, as if coming out of a vast distance—but, even so, infinitely appalling, reached the ear.

There were signs of a hideous commotion all over the house: lights passed along and up, doors opened and shut and running figures passed within the windows. The clock in the stable turret tolled one, and darkness fell again.

It was only dispelled once more, to show the house front. At the bottom of the steps, dark figures were drawn up in two lines, holding flaming torches. More dark figures came down the steps, bearing, first one, then another small coffin. And the lines of torch-bearers with the coffins between them moved silently onward to the left.

The hours of the night passed on—never so slowly, Mr Dillet thought. Gradually he sank from sitting to lying in his bed—but he did not close an eye: and early next morning he sent for the doctor.

The doctor found him in a disquieting state of nerves and recommended sea air to a quiet place on the East Coast.

One of the first people he met on the seafront was Mr Chittenden, who, it appeared, had likewise been advised to take his wife away for a bit of a change.

Mr Chittenden looked somewhat askance upon him when they met: and not without cause.

'Well, I don't wonder at you being a bit upset, Mr Dillet. What? Yes, well, I might say 'orrible upset, to be sure, seeing what me and my poor wife went through ourselves. But I put it to you, Mr Dillet, one of two things: was I going to scrap a lovely piece like that on the one 'and, or was I going to tell customers: "I'm selling you a regular picture-palace-dramar in reel life of the olden time, billed to perform regular at one o'clock a.m.?" Why, what would you 'ave said yourself? And next thing you know, two Justices of the Peace in the back parlour, and pore Mr and Mrs Chittenden off in a spring cart to the County Asylum and everyone in the street saying, "Ah, I thought it 'ud come to that. Look at the way the man drank!"—and me next door, or next door but one, to a total abstainer, as you know. Well, there was my position. What? Me 'ave it back in the shop? Well, what doyou think? No, but I'll tell you what I will do. You shall have your money back, bar the ten pound I paid for it, and you make what you can.'

Later in the day, in what is offensively called the 'smoke room' of the hotel, a murmured conversation between the two went on for some time.

'How much do you really know about that thing, and where it came from?'

'Honest, Mr Dillet, I don't know the 'ouse. Of course, it came out of the lumber room of a country 'ouse—that anyone could guess. But I'll go as far as to say this, that I believe it's not a hundred miles from this place. Which direction and how far I've no notion. I'm only judging by guesswork. The man I actually paid the cheque to ain't one of my regular men and I've lost sight of him. But I 'ave the idea that this part of the country was his beat, and that's every word I can tell you. But now, Mr Dillet, there's one thing that rather physicks me—that old chap,—I suppose you saw him drive up to the door—I thought so: now, would he have been the medical man, do you take it? My wife would have it so, but I stuck to it that was the lawyer, because he had papers with him, and one he took out was folded up.'

'I agree,' said Mr Dillet. 'Thinking it over, I came to the conclusion that was the old man's will, ready to be signed.'

'Just what I thought,' said Mr Chittenden, 'and I took it that will would have cut out the young people, eh? Well, well! It's been a lesson to me, I know that. I shan't buy no more dolls' houses, nor waste no more money on the pictures—and as to this business of poisonin' grandpa, well, if I know myself, I never 'ad much of a turn for that. Live and let live: that's been my motto throughout life, and I ain't found it a bad one.'

Filled with these elevated sentiments, Mr Chittenden retired to his lodgings. Mr Dillet next day repaired to the local Institute, where he hoped to find some clue to the riddle that absorbed him. He gazed in despair at a long file of the Canterbury and York Society's publications of the Parish Registers of the district. No print resembling the house of his nightmare was among those that hung on the staircase and in the passages. Disconsolate, he found himself at last in a derelict room, staring at a dusty model of a church in a dusty glass case: Model of St Stephen's Church, Coxham. Presented by J. Merewether, Esq., of Ilbridge House, 1877. The work of his ancestor James Merewether, d. 1786. There was something in the fashion of it that reminded him dimly of his horror. He retraced his steps to a wall map he had noticed and made out that Ilbridge House was in Coxham Parish. Coxham was, as it happened, one of the parishes of which he had retained the name when he glanced over the file of printed registers, and it was not long before he found in them the record of the burial of Roger Milford, aged 76, on the 11 September 1757, and of Roger and Elizabeth Merewether, aged nine and seven, on the 19th of the same month. It seemed worthwhile to follow up on this clue, frail as it was; and in the afternoon he drove out to Coxham. The east end of the north aisle of the church is a Milford chapel, and on its north wall are tablets to the same persons; Roger, the elder, it seems, was distinguished by all the qualities which adorn 'the Father, the Magistrate and the Man'. The memorial was erected by his attached daughter Elizabeth, 'who did not long survive the loss of a parent ever solicitous for her welfare, and of two amiable children.' The last sentence was plainly an addition to the original inscription.

A yet later slab told of James Merewether, husband of Elizabeth, 'who in the dawn of life practised, not without success, those arts which, had he continued their exercise, might in the opinion of the most competent judges have earned for him the name of the British Vitruvius: but who, overwhelmed by the visitation which deprived him of an affectionate partner and a blooming offspring, passed his Prime and Age in a secluded yet elegant Retirement: his grateful Nephew and Heir indulges a pious sorrow by this too brief recital of his excellences.'

The children were more simply commemorated. Both died on the night of 12 September.

Mr Dillet felt sure that in Ilbridge House he had found the scene of his drama. In some old sketch-book, possibly in some old print, he may yet find convincing evidence that he is right. But the Ilbridge House of today is not that which he sought; it is an Elizabethan erection of the forties, in red brick with stone quoins and dressings. A quarter of a mile from it, in a low part of the park, backed by ancient, stag-horned, ivy-strangled trees and thick undergrowth, are marks of a terraced platform overgrown with rough grass. A few stone balusters lie here and there, and a heap or two, covered with nettles and ivy, of wrought stones with badly carved crockets. This, someone told Mr Dillet, was the site of an older house.

As he drove out of the village, the hall clock struck four, and Mr Dillet started up and clapped his hands to his ears. It was not the first time he had heard that bell.

Awaiting an offer from the other side of the Atlantic, the doll's house still reposes, carefully sheeted, in a loft over Mr Dillet's stables, whither Collins conveyed it on the day when Mr Dillet started for the sea coast.

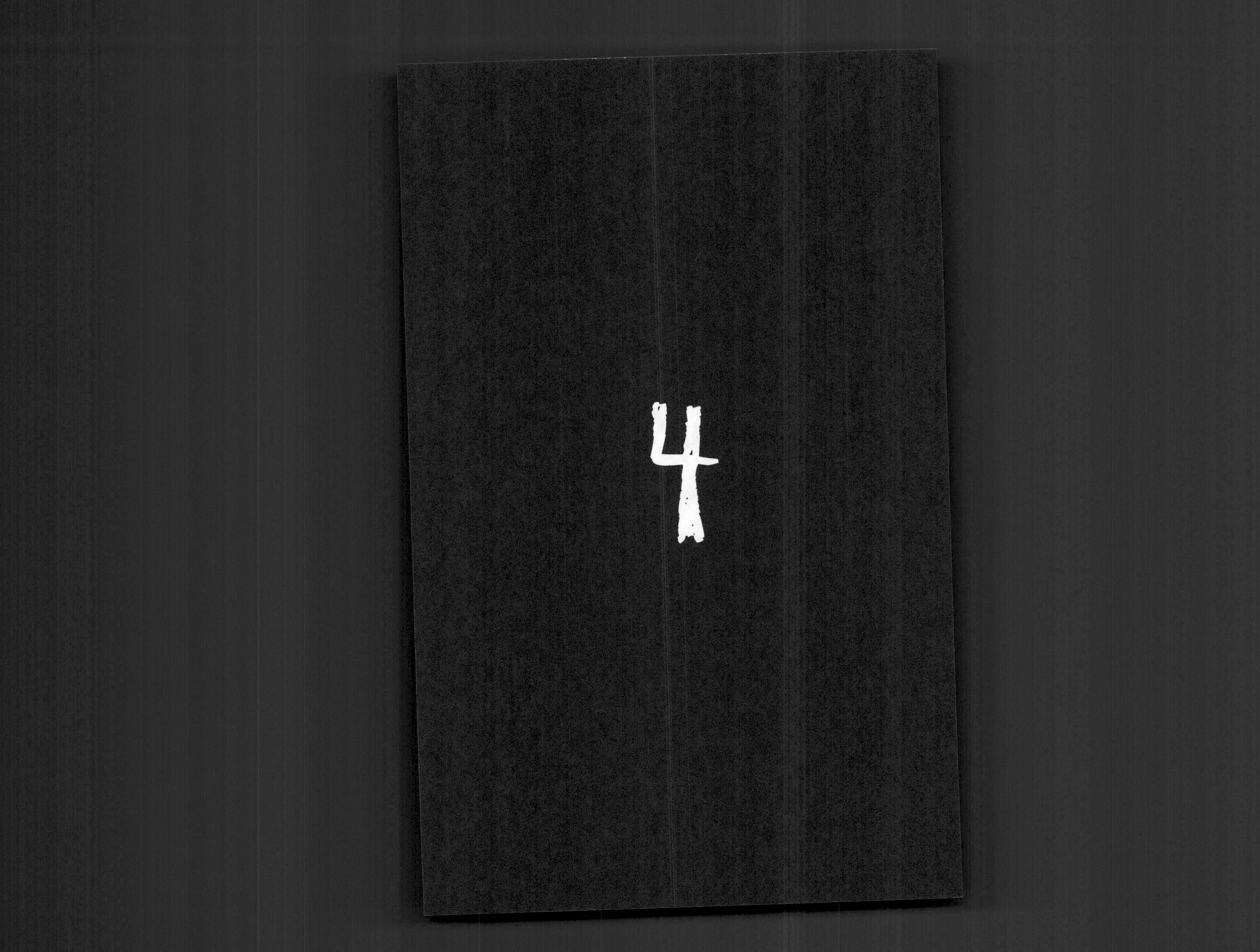

4

My Own True Ghost Story

Rudyard Kipling

*My Own True Ghost Story
As I came through the Desert thus it was—
As I came through the Desert.
The City of Dreadful Night.*

Somewhere in the Other World, where there are books and pictures and plays and shop windows to look at and thousands of men who spend their lives building up all four, lives a gentleman who writes real stories about the real insides of people; and his name is Mr. Walter Besant. But he will insist upon treating his ghosts— he has published half a workshop full of them—with levity. He makes his ghost-seers talk familiarly, and, in some cases, flirt outrageously, with the phantoms. You may treat anything, from a Viceroy to a Vernacular Paper, with levity; but you must behave reverently toward a ghost, and particularly an Indian one.

There are, in this land, ghosts who take the form of fat, cold, pobby corpses, and hide in trees near the roadside till a traveller passes. Then they drop upon his neck and remain. There are also terrible ghosts of women who have died in childbirth. These wander along the pathways at dusk or hide in the crops near a village, and call seductively. But to answer their call is death in this world and the next. Their feet are turned backwards so that all sober men may recognise them. There are ghosts of little children who have been thrown into wells. These haunt well curbs and the fringes of jungles, and wail under the stars, or catch women by the wrist and beg to be taken up and carried. These and the corpse ghosts, however, are only vernacular articles and do not attack Sahibs. No native ghost has yet been authentically reported to have frightened an Englishman, but many English ghosts have scared the life out of both white and black.

Nearly every other Station owns a ghost. There are said to be two at Simla, not counting the woman who blows the bellows at Syree dak-bungalow on the Old Road. Mussoorie has a house haunted by a very lively Thing. A white lady is supposed to do night-watchman round a house in Lahore. Dalhousie says that one of her houses 'repeats' on autumn evenings all the incidents of a horrible horse and precipice accident. Murree has a merry ghost, and, now that she has been swept by cholera, will have room for a sorrowful one. There are Officers' Quarters in Mian Mir whose doors open without reason, and whose furniture is guaranteed to creak, not with the heat of June but with the weight of Invisibles who come to lounge in the chairs. Peshawar possesses houses that none will willingly rent; and there is something—not fever—wrong with a big bungalow in Allahabad. The older Provinces simply bristle with haunted houses, and march phantom armies along their main thoroughfares.

Some of the dak-bungalows on the Grand Trunk Road have handy little cemeteries in their compound— witnesses to the 'changes and chances of this mortal life' in the days when men drove from Calcutta to the Northwest. These bungalows are objectionable places to put up in. They are generally very old and always dirty, while the khansamah is as ancient as the bungalow. He either chatters senilely or falls into the long trances of age. In both moods he is useless. If you get angry with him, he refers to some Sahib dead and buried these thirty years, and says that when he was in that Sahib's service not a khansamah in the province could touch him. Then he jabbers and mows and trembles and fidgets among the dishes, and you repent of your irritation.

In these dak-bungalows, ghosts are most likely to be found, and when found, they should be made a note of. Not long ago it was my business to live in dak-bungalows. I never inhabited the same house for three nights running and grew to be learned in the breed. I lived in Government-built ones with red brick walls and rail ceilings, an inventory of the furniture posted in every room, and an excited snake at the threshold to give a welcome. I lived in 'converted' ones—old houses officiating as dak-bungalows—where nothing was in its proper place and there wasn't even a fowl for dinner. I lived in second-hand palaces where the wind blew through open-work marble tracery just as uncomfortably as through a broken pane.

I lived in Dak bungalows where the last entry in the visitors' book was fifteen months old, and where they slashed off the curry kid's head with a sword. It was my good luck to meet all sorts of men, from sober travelling missionaries and deserters flying from British Regiments, to drunken loafers who threw whisky bottles at all who passed; and my still greater good fortune just to escape a maternity case. Seeing that a fair proportion of the tragedy of our lives out here acted itself in dak-bungalows, I wondered that I had met no ghosts. A ghost that would voluntarily hang about a dak-bungalow would be mad of course. But so many men have died mad in dak-bungalows that there must be a fair percentage of lunatic ghosts.

In due time I found my ghost, or ghosts rather, for there were two of them. Up till that hour, I had sympathised with Mr Besant's method of handling them, as shown in The Strange Case of Mr Lucraft and Other Stories. I am now in the Opposition.

We will call the bungalow Katmal dak-bungalow. But THAT was the smallest part of the horror. A man with a sensitive hide has no right to sleep in dak-bungalows. He should marry. Katmal dak- bungalow was old and rotten and unrepaired. The floor was of worn brick, the walls were filthy, and the windows were nearly black with grime. It stood on a bypath largely used by native Sub-Deputy Assistants of all kinds, from Finance to Forests; but real Sahibs were rare. The khansamah, who was nearly bent double with old age, said so.

When I arrived, there was a fitful, undecided rain on the face of the land, accompanied by a restless wind, and every gust made a noise like the rattling of dry bones in the stiff toddy palms outside. The khansamah completely lost his head on my arrival. He had served a Sahib once. Did I know that, Sahib? He gave me the name of a well-known man who has been buried for more than a quarter of a century and showed me an ancient daguerreotype of that man in his prehistoric youth. I had seen a steel engraving of him at the head of a double volume of Memoirs a month before, and I felt ancient beyond telling.

The day shut in and the khansamah went to get me food. He did not go through the pretence of calling it 'khana'—man's victuals. He said 'ratub,' and that means, among other things, 'grub'—dog's rations. There was no insult in his choice of the term. He had forgotten the other word, I suppose.

While he was cutting up the dead bodies of animals, I settled myself down, after exploring the dak-bungalow. There were three rooms, beside my own, which was a corner kennel, each giving into the other through dingy white doors fastened with long iron bars. The bungalow was a very solid one, but the partition walls of the rooms were almost jerry-built in their flimsiness. Every step or bang of a trunk echoed from my room down the other three, and every footfall came back tremulously from the far walls. For this reason, I shut the door. There were no lamps—only candles in long glass shades. An oil wick was set in the bathroom.

For bleak, unadulterated misery that dak-bungalow was the worst of the many that I had ever set foot in. There was no fireplace, and the windows would not open; so a brazier of charcoal would have been useless. The rain and the wind splashed and gurgled and moaned around the house, and the toddy palms rattled and roared. Half a dozen jackals went through the compound singing, and a hyena stood afar off and mocked them. A hyena would convince a Sadducee of the Resurrection of the Dead— the worst sort of Dead. Then came the ratub—a curious meal, half native and half English in composition—with the old khansamah babbling behind my chair about dead and gone English people, and the wind-blown candles playing shadow-bo-peep with the bed and the mosquito curtains. It was just the sort of dinner and evening to make a man think of every single one of his past sins, and of all the others that he intended to commit if he lived.

Sleep, for several hundred reasons, was not easy. The lamp in the bathroom threw the most absurd shadows into the room, and the wind was beginning to talk nonsense.

Just when the reasons were drowsy with blood-sucking I heard the regular—'Let—us—take—and—heave—him—over' grunt of doolie-bearers in the compound. First one doolie came in, then a second, and then a third. I heard the doolies dumped on the ground, and the shutter in front of my door shook. 'That's someone trying to come in,' I said. But no one spoke, and I persuaded myself that it was the gusty wind. The shutter of the room next to mine was attacked, flung back, and the inner door opened. 'That's some Sub-Deputy Assistant,' I said, 'and he has brought his friends with him. Now they'll talk and spit and smoke for an hour.'

But there were no voices and no footsteps. No one was putting his luggage into the next room. The door shut, and I thanked Providence that I was to be left in peace. But I was curious to know where the doolies had gone. I got out of bed and looked into the darkness. There was never a sign of a doolie. Just as I was getting into bed again, I heard, in the next room, the sound that no man in his senses can possibly mistake—the whir of a billiard ball down the length of the slates when the striker is stringing for break. No other sound is like it. A minute afterwards there was another whir, and I got into bed. I was not frightened—indeed I was not. I was very curious to know what had become of the doolies. I jumped into bed for that reason.

Next minute I heard the double click of a cannon and my hair sat up. It is a mistake to say that hair stands up. The skin of the head tightens and you can feel a faint, prickly, bristling all over the scalp. That is the hair sitting up.

There was a whir and a click, and both sounds could only have been made by one thing—a billiard ball. I argued the matter out at great length with myself; and the more I argued the less probable it seemed that one bed, one table, and two chairs—all the furniture of the room next to mine—could so exactly duplicate the sounds of a game of billiards. After another cannon, a three-cushion one to judge by the whir, I argued no more. I had found my ghost and would have given worlds to have escaped from that dak- bungalow. I listened, and with each listen the game grew clearer. There was whir on whir and click on click. Sometimes there was a double click and a whir and another click. Beyond any sort of doubt, people were playing billiards in the next room. And the next room was not big enough to hold a billiard table!

Between the pauses of the wind, I heard the game go forward—stroke after stroke. I tried to believe that I could not hear voices. But that attempt was a failure.

Do you know what fear is? Not ordinary fear of insult, injury or death, but abject, quivering dread of something that you cannot see—fear that dries the inside of the mouth and half of the throat—fear that makes you sweat on the palms of the hands, and gulp in order to keep the uvula at work? This is a fine Fear—great cowardice and must be felt to be appreciated. The very improbability of billiards in a dak-bungalow proved the reality of the thing. No man—drunk or sober—could imagine a game at billiards, or invent the spitting crack of a 'screw-cannon.'

A severe course of dak-bungalows has this disadvantage—it breeds infinite credulity. If a man said to a confirmed dak bungalow haunter, 'There is a corpse in the next room, and there's a mad girl in the next but one, and the woman and man on that camel have just eloped from a place sixty miles away,' the hearer would not disbelieve because he would know that nothing is too wild, grotesque, or horrible to happen in a dak-bungalow.

This credulity, unfortunately, extends to ghosts. A rational person fresh from his own house would have turned on his side and slept. I did not. So surely as I was given up as a bad carcass by the scores of things in the bed because the bulk of my blood was in my heart, so surely did I hear every stroke of a long game at billiards played in the echoing room behind the iron-barred door. My dominant fear was that the players might want a marker. It was an absurd fear; because creatures who could play in the dark would be above such superfluities. I only know that that was my terror. And it was real.

After a long, long while the game stopped, and the door banged. I slept because I was dead tired. Otherwise,

I should have preferred to have kept awake. Not for everything in Asia would I have dropped the door bar and peered into the dark of the next room.

When the morning came, I considered that I had done well and wisely, and inquired for the means of departure.

'By the way, khansamah,' I said, 'what were those three doolies doing in my compound in the night?'

'There were no doolies,' said the khansamah.

I went into the next room and the daylight streamed through the open door. I was immensely brave. I would, at that hour, have played Black Pool with the owner of the big Black Pool down below.

'Has this place always been a dak-bungalow?' I asked.

'No,' said the khansamah. 'Ten or twenty years ago, I have forgotten how long, it was a billiard room.'

'A how much?'

'A billiard room for the Sahibs who built the Railway. I was khansamah then in the big house where all the Railway-Sahibs lived, and I used to come across with brandy-shrab. These three rooms were all one, and they held a big table on which the Sahibs played every evening. But the Sahibs are all dead now, and the Railway runs, you say, nearly to Kabul.'

'Do you remember anything about the Sahibs?'

'It is long ago, but I remember that one Sahib, a fat man and always angry, was playing here one night, and he said to me, "Mangal Khan, brandy-pani do," and I filled the glass, and he bent over the table to strike, and his head fell lower and lower till it hit the table, and his spectacles came off, and when we—the Sahibs and I myself—ran to lift him, he was dead. I helped to carry him out. Aha, he was a strong Sahib! But he is dead and I, old Mangal Khan, am still living, by your favour.'

That was more than enough! I had my ghost—a firsthand, authenticated article. I would write to the Society for Psychical Research—I would paralyse the Empire with the news! But I would, first of all, put eighty miles of assessed crop land between myself and that dak-bungalow before nightfall. The Society might send their regular agent to investigate later on.

I went into my own room and prepared to pack after noting down the facts of the case. As I smoked, I heard the game begin again. The door was open and I could see into the room. Click ... click! That was a cannon. I entered the room without fear, for there was sunlight within and a fresh breeze without. The unseen game was going on at a tremendous rate. And well it might, when a restless little rat was running to and fro inside the dingy ceiling cloth, and a piece of loose window-sash was making fifty breaks off the window bolt as it shook in the breeze!

Impossible to mistake the sound of billiard balls! Impossible to mistake the whir of a ball over the slate! But I was to be excused. Even when I shut my enlightened eyes the sound was marvelously like that of a fast game.

Entered angrily the faithful partner of my sorrows, Kadir Baksh.

'This bungalow is very bad and low-caste! No wonder the Presence was disturbed and is speckled. Three sets of doolie-bearers came to the bungalow late last night when I was sleeping outside, and said that it was their custom to rest in the rooms set apart for the English people! What honour has the khansamah? They tried to enter, but I told them to go. No wonder, if these Oorias have been here, that the Presence is sorely spotted. It is shame, and the work of a dirty man!'

Kadir Baksh did not say that he had taken from each gang two annas for rent in advance, and then, beyond my earshot, had beaten them with the big green umbrella whose use I could never before divine. But Kadir Baksh has no notions of morality.

There was an interview with the khansamah, but as he promptly lost his head, wrath gave place to pity, and pity led to a long conversation, in the course of which he put the fat Engineer-Sahib's tragic death in three separate stations—two of them fifty miles away. The third shift was to Calcutta, and there the Sahib died while driving a dogcart.

If I had encouraged him the khansamah would have wandered all through Bengal with his corpse.

I did not go away as soon as I intended. I stayed for the night, while the wind and the rat and the sash and the window bolt played a ding-dong 'hundred and fifty up.' Then the wind ran out and the billiards stopped, and I felt that I had ruined my one genuine, hallmarked ghost story.

Had I only stopped at the proper time, I could have made ANYTHING out of it.

That was the bitterest thought of all!

5

The Shadows on the Wall

Mary Eleanor Wilkins Freeman

'Henry had words with Edward in the study the night before Edward died,' said Caroline Glynn.

She spoke not with acrimony, but with grave severity. Rebecca Ann Glynn gasped by way of assent. She sat in a wide flounce of black silk in the corner of the sofa and rolled terrified eyes from her sister Caroline to her sister Mrs Stephen Brigham, who had been Emma Glynn, the one beauty of the family. The latter was beautiful still, with a large, splendid, full-blown beauty, she filled a great rocking chair with her superb bulk of femininity, and swayed gently back and forth, her black silks whispering and her black frills fluttering. Even the shock of death—for her brother Edward lay dead in the house—could not disturb her outward serenity of demeanour.

But even her expression of masterly placidity changed before her sister Caroline's announcement and her sister Rebecca Ann's gasp of terror and distress in response.

'I think Henry might have controlled his temper when poor Edward was so near his end,' she said with an asperity which disturbed slightly the roseate curves of her beautiful mouth.

'Of course, he did not know,' murmured Rebecca Ann in a faint tone.

'Of course, he did not know it,' said Caroline quickly. She turned on her sister with a strange, sharp look of suspicion. Then she shrank as if from the other's possible answer.

Rebecca gasped again. The married sister, Mrs Emma Brigham, was now sitting up straight in her chair; she had ceased rocking and was eyeing them both intently with a sudden accentuation of family likeness on her face.

'What do you mean?' said she impartially to them both. Then she, too, seemed to shrink before a possible answer. She even laughed an evasive sort of laugh.

'Nobody means anything,' said Caroline firmly. She rose and crossed the room toward the door with grim decisiveness.

'Where are you going?' asked Mrs Brigham.

'I have something to see to,' replied Caroline, and the others at once knew by her tone that she had some solemn and sad duty to perform in the chamber of death.

'Oh,' said Mrs Brigham.

After the door had closed behind Caroline, she turned to Rebecca.

'Did Henry have many words with him?' she asked.

'They were talking very loud,' replied Rebecca evasively.

Mrs Brigham looked at her. She had not resumed rocking. She still sat up straight, with a slight knitting of intensity on her fair forehead, between the pretty rippling curves of her auburn hair.

'Did you—ever hear anything?' she asked in a low voice with a glance toward the door.

'I was just across the hall in the south parlour, and that door was open and this door ajar,' replied Rebecca with a slight flush.

'Then you must have—'

'I couldn't help it.'

'Everything?'

'Most of it.'

'What was it?'

'The old story.'

'I suppose Henry was mad, as he always was, because Edward was living on here for nothing when he had wasted all the money father left him.'

Rebecca nodded, with a fearful glance at the door.

When Emma spoke again her voice was still more hushed. 'I know how he felt,' said she. 'It must have looked to him as if Edward was living at his expense, but he wasn't.'

'No, he wasn't.'

'And Edward had a right here according to the terms of father's will, and Henry ought to have remembered it.'

'Yes, he ought.'

'Did he say hard things?'

'Pretty hard, from what I heard.'

'What?'

'I heard him tell Edward that he had no business here at all, and he thought he had better go away.'

'What did Edward say?'

'That he would stay here as long as he lived and afterwards, too, if he was a mind to, and he would like to see Henry get him out; and then—'

'What?'

'Then he laughed.'

'What did Henry say?'

'I didn't hear him say anything, but—'

'But what?'

'I saw him when he came out of this room.'

'He looked mad?'

'You've seen him when he looked so.'

Emma nodded. The expression of horror on her face had deepened.

'Do you remember that time he killed the cat because she had scratched him?'

'Yes. Don't!'

Then Caroline reentered the room; she went up to the stove, in which a wood fire was burning—it was a cold, gloomy day of fall—and she warmed her hands, which were reddened from recent washing in cold water.

Mrs Brigham looked at her and hesitated. She glanced at the door, which was still ajar; it did not easily shut, being still swollen with the damp weather of the summer. She rose and pushed it together with a sharp thud, which jarred the house. Rebecca started painfully with a half-exclamation. Caroline looked at her disapprovingly.

'It is time you controlled your nerves, Rebecca,' she said.

Mrs Brigham, returning from the closed door, said imperiously that it ought to be fixed, it shut so hard.

'It will shrink enough after we have had the fire a few days,' replied Caroline.

'I think Henry ought to be ashamed of himself for talking as he did to Edward,' said Mrs Brigham abruptly, but in an almost inaudible voice.

'Hush,' said Caroline, with a glance of actual fear at the closed door.

'Nobody can hear with the door shut. I say again I think Henry ought to be ashamed of himself. I shouldn't think he'd ever get over it, having words with poor Edward the very night before he died. Edward was enough sight better disposition than Henry, with all his faults.'

'I never heard him speak a cross word, unless he spoke cross to Henry that last night. I don't know but he did from what Rebecca overheard.'

'Not so much cross, as sort of soft, and sweet, and aggravating,' sniffed Rebecca.

'What do you really think ailed Edward?' asked Emma in hardly more than a whisper. She did not look at her sister.

'I know you said that he had terrible pains in his stomach, and had spasms, but what do you think made him have them?'

'Henry called it gastric trouble. You know Edward has always had dyspepsia.'

Mrs Brigham hesitated a moment. 'Was there any talk of an—examination?' said she.

Then Caroline turned on her fiercely.

'No,' said she in a terrible voice. 'No.'

The three sisters' souls seemed to meet on one common ground of terrified understanding through their eyes.

The old-fashioned latch of the door was heard to rattle, and a push from without made the door shake ineffectually. 'It's Henry,' Rebecca sighed rather than whispered. Mrs Brigham settled herself, after a noiseless rush across the floor, into her rocking chair again, and was swaying back and forth with her head comfortably leaning back, when the door at last yielded and Henry Glynn entered. He cast a covertly sharp, comprehensive glance at Mrs Brigham with her elaborate calm, at Rebecca quietly huddled in the corner of the sofa with her handkerchief to her face and only one small uncovered reddened ear as attentive as a dog's and at Caroline sitting with a strained composure in her armchair by the stove. She met his eyes quite firmly with a look of inscrutable fear, and defiance of the fear and him.

Henry Glynn looked more like this sister than the others. Both had the same hard delicacy of form and aquilinity of feature. They confronted each other with the pitiless immovability of two statues in whose marble lineaments emotions were fixed for all eternity.

Then Henry Glynn smiled and the smile transformed his face. He looked suddenly years younger, and an almost boyish recklessness appeared in his face. He flung himself into a chair with a gesture which was bewildering from its incongruity with his general appearance. He leaned his head back, flung one leg over the other, and looked laughingly at Mrs Brigham.

'I declare, Emma, you grow younger every year,' he said.

She flushed a little, and her placid mouth widened at the corners. She was susceptible to praise.

'Our thoughts today ought to belong to the one of us who will never grow older,' said Caroline in a hard voice.

Henry looked at her, still smiling. 'Of course, we none of us forget that,' said he, in a deep, gentle voice; 'but we have to speak to the living, Caroline, and I have not seen Emma for a long time, and the living are as dear as the dead.'

'Not to me,' said Caroline.

She rose and went abruptly out of the room again. Rebecca also rose and hurried after her, sobbing loudly.

Henry looked slowly after them.

'Caroline is completely unstrung,' said he.

Mrs Brigham rocked. A confidence in him inspired by his manner was stealing over her. Out of that confidence, she spoke quite easily and naturally.

'His death was very sudden,' said she.

Henry's eyelids quivered slightly but his gaze was unswerving.

'Yes,' said he, 'it was very sudden. He was sick only a few hours.'

'What did you call it?'

'Gastric.'

'You did not think of an examination?'

'There was no need. I am perfectly certain as to the cause of his death.'

Suddenly Mrs Brigham felt a creep as of some live horror over her very soul. Her flesh prickled with cold, before an inflexion of his voice. She rose, tottering on weak knees.

'Where are you going?' asked Henry in a strange, breathless voice.

Mrs Brigham said something incoherent about some sewing which she had to do—some black for the funeral—and was out of the room. She went up to the front chamber which she occupied. Caroline was there.

She went close to her and took her hands, and the two sisters looked at each other.

'Don't speak, don't, I won't have it!' said Caroline finally in an awful whisper.

'I won't,' replied Emma.

That afternoon the three sisters were in the study.

Mrs Brigham was hemming some black material. At last, she laid her work on her lap.

'It's no use, I cannot see to sew another stitch until we have a light,' said she.

Caroline, who was writing some letters at the table, turned to Rebecca, in her usual place on the sofa.

'Rebecca, you had better get a lamp,' she said.

Rebecca started up; even in the dusk, her face showed her agitation.

'It doesn't seem to me that we need a lamp quite yet,' she said in a piteous, pleading voice like a child's.

'Yes, we do,' returned Mrs Brigham peremptorily. 'I can't see to sew another stitch.'

Rebecca rose and left the room. Presently she entered with a lamp. She set it on the table, an old-fashioned card table which was placed against the opposite wall from the window. That opposite wall was taken up with three doors; the one small space was occupied by the table.

'What have you put that lamp over there for?' asked Mrs Brigham, with more impatience than her voice usually revealed. 'Why didn't you set it in the hall, and have done with it? Neither Caroline nor I can see if it is on that table.'

'I thought perhaps you would move,' replied Rebecca hoarsely.

'If I do move, we can't both sit at that table. Caroline has her paper all spread around. Why don't you set the lamp on the study table in the middle of the room, then we can both see?'

Rebecca hesitated. Her face was very pale. She looked with an appeal that was fairly agonizing at her sister Caroline.

'Why don't you put the lamp on this table, as she says?' asked Caroline, almost fiercely. 'Why do you act so, Rebecca?'

Rebecca took the lamp and set it on the table in the middle of the room without another word. Then she seated herself on the sofa and placed a hand over her eyes as if to shade them, and remained so.

'Does the light hurt your eyes, and is that the reason why you didn't want the lamp?' asked Mrs Brigham kindly.

'I always like to sit in the dark,' replied Rebecca chokingly. Then she snatched her handkerchief hastily from her pocket and began to weep. Caroline continued to write, Mrs Brigham to sew.

Suddenly Mrs Brigham as she sewed glanced at the opposite wall. The glance became a steady stare. She looked intently; her work suspended in her hands. Then she looked away again and took a few more stitches, then she looked again and again turned to her task. At last, she laid her work in her lap and stared concentratedly. She looked from the wall around the room, taking note of the various objects. Then she turned to her sisters.

'What is that?' said she.

'What?' asked Caroline harshly.

'That strange shadow on the wall,' replied Mrs Brigham.

Rebecca sat with her face hidden; Caroline dipped her pen in the inkstand.

'Why don't you turn around and look?' asked Mrs Brigham in a wondering and somewhat aggrieved way.

'I am in a hurry to finish this letter,' replied Caroline shortly.

Mrs Brigham rose, her work slipping to the floor, and began walking around the room, moving various articles of furniture, with her eyes on the shadow.

Then suddenly she shrieked out:

'Look at this awful shadow! What is it? Caroline, look, look! Rebecca, look! What is it?'

All Mrs Brigham's triumphant placidity was gone. Her handsome face was livid with horror. She stood stiffly pointing at the shadow.

Then after a shuddering glance at the wall, Rebecca burst out in a wild wail.

'Oh, Caroline, there it is again, there it is again!'

'Caroline Glynn, you look!' said Mrs Brigham. 'Look! What is that dreadful shadow?'

Caroline rose, turned, and stood confronting the wall.

'How should I know?' she said.

'It has been there every night since he died!' cried Rebecca.

'Every night?'

'Yes; he died Thursday and this is Saturday; that makes three nights,' said Caroline rigidly. She stood as if holding her calm with a vise of concentrated will.

'It—it looks like—like—' stammered Mrs Brigham in a tone of intense horror.

'I know what it looks like well enough,' said Caroline. 'I've got eyes in my head.'

'It looks like Edward,' burst out Rebecca in a sort of frenzy of fear. 'Only——'

'Yes, it does,' assented Mrs Brigham, whose horror-stricken tone matched her sisters', 'only—Oh, it is awful! What is it, Caroline?'

'I ask you again, how should I know?' replied Caroline. 'I see it there like you. How should I know any more than you?'

'It must be something in the room,' said Mrs Brigham, staring wildly around.

'We moved everything in the room the first night it came,' said Rebecca; 'it is not anything in the room.'

Caroline turned upon her with a sort of fury. 'Of course, it is something in the room,' said she. 'How you act! What do you mean talking so? Of course, it is something in the room.'

'Of course, it is,' agreed Mrs Brigham, looking at Caroline suspiciously. 'It must be something in the room.'

'It is not anything in the room,' repeated Rebecca with obstinate horror.

The door opened suddenly and Henry Glynn entered. He began to speak, then his eyes followed the direction of the others. He stood staring at the shadow on the wall.

'What is that?' he demanded in a strange voice.

'It must be due to something in the room,' Mrs Brigham said faintly.

Henry Glynn stood and stared a moment longer. His face showed a gamut of emotions. Horror, conviction, then furious incredulity. Suddenly he began hastening hither and thither about the room. He moved the furniture with fierce jerks, turning ever to see the effect upon the shadow on the wall. Not a line of its terrible outlines wavered.

'It must be something in the room!' he declared in a voice which seemed to snap like a lash.

His face changed, the inmost secrecy of his nature seemed evident upon his face until one almost lost sight of his lineaments. Rebecca stood close to her sofa, regarding him with woeful, fascinated eyes. Mrs Brigham clutched Caroline's hand. They both stood in a corner out of his way. For a few moments, he raged about the room like a caged wild animal. He moved every piece of furniture; when the moving of a piece did not affect the shadow, he flung it to the floor.

Then suddenly he desisted. He laughed.

'What an absurdity,' he said easily. 'Such a to-do about a shadow.'

'That's so,' assented Mrs Brigham, in a scared voice which she tried to make natural. As she spoke, she lifted a chair near her.

'I think you have broken the chair that Edward was fond of,' said Caroline.

Terror and wrath were struggling for expression on her face. Her mouth was set, her eyes shrinking. Henry lifted the chair with a show of anxiety.

'Just as good as ever,' he said pleasantly. He laughed again, looking at his sisters. 'Did I scare you?' he said. 'I should think you might be used to me by this time. You know my way of wanting to leap to the bottom of a mystery, and that shadow does look—queer, like—and I thought if there was any way of accounting for it I would like to without any delay.'

'You don't seem to have succeeded,' remarked Caroline dryly, with a slight glance at the wall.

Henry's eyes followed hers and he quivered perceptibly.

'Oh, there is no accounting for shadows,' he said, and he laughed again. 'A man is a fool to try to account for shadows.'

Then the supper bell rang, and they all left the room, but Henry kept his back to the wall—as did, indeed, the others.

Henry led the way with an alert motion like a boy; Rebecca brought up the rear. She could scarcely walk, her knees trembled so.

'I can't sit in that room again this evening,' she whispered to Caroline after supper.

'Very well; we will sit in the south room,' replied Caroline. 'I think we will sit in the south parlour,' she said aloud; 'it isn't as damp as the study, and I have a cold.'

So, they all sat in the south room with their sewing. Henry read the newspaper; his chair drawn close to the lamp on the table. About nine o'clock he rose abruptly and crossed the hall to the study. The three sisters looked at one another. Mrs Brigham rose, folded her rustling skirts compactly around her, and began tiptoeing toward the door.

'What are you going to do?' inquired Rebecca agitatedly.

'I am going to see what he is about,' replied Mrs Brigham cautiously.

As she spoke, she pointed to the study door across the hall; it was ajar. Henry had striven to pull it together behind him, but it had somehow swollen beyond the limit with curious speed. It was still ajar and a streak of light showed from top to bottom.

Mrs Brigham folded her skirts so tightly that her bulk with its swelling curves was revealed in a black silk sheath, and she went with a slow toddle across the hall to the study door. She stood there, her eye at the crack.

In the south room, Rebecca stopped sewing and sat watching with dilated eyes. Caroline sewed steadily. What Mrs Brigham, standing at the crack in the study door, saw was this:

Henry Glynn, evidently reasoning that the source of the strange shadow must be between the table on which the lamp stood and the wall, was making systematic passes and thrusts with an old sword which had belonged to his father all over and through the intervening space. Not an inch was left unpierced. He seemed to have divided the space into mathematical sections. He brandished the sword with a sort of cold fury and calculation; the blade gave out flashes of light and the shadow remained unmoved. Mrs Brigham, watching, felt herself cold with horror.

Finally, Henry ceased and stood with the sword in hand and raised as if to strike, surveying the shadow on the wall threateningly. Mrs Brigham toddled back across the hall and shut the south room door behind her before she related what she had seen.

'He looked like a demon,' she said again. 'Have you got any of that old wine in the house, Caroline? I don't feel as if I could stand much more.'

'Yes, there's plenty,' said Caroline; 'you can have some when you go to bed.'

'I think we had all better take some,' said Mrs Brigham. 'Oh, Caroline, what——'

'Don't ask. Don't speak,' said Caroline.

'No, I'm not going to,' replied Mrs Brigham, 'but—'

Soon the three sisters went to their chambers and the south parlour was deserted. Caroline called to Henry in the study to put out the light before he came upstairs. They had been gone about an hour when he came into the room bringing the lamp which had stood in the study. He set it on the table, and waited a few minutes, pacing up and down. His face was terrible, his fair complexion showed livid, and his blue eyes seemed dark blanks of awful reflections.

Then he took up the lamp and returned to the library. He set the lamp on the center table and the shadow sprang out on the wall. Again, he studied the furniture and moved it about, but deliberately, with none of his former frenzy. Nothing affected the shadow. Then he returned to the south room with the lamp and again waited. Again, he returned to the study and placed the lamp on the table, and the shadow sprang out upon the wall. It was midnight before he went upstairs. Mrs Brigham and the other sisters, who could not sleep, heard him.

The next day was the funeral. That evening the family sat in the south room. Some relatives were with them. Nobody entered the study until Henry carried a lamp in there after the others had retired for the night. He saw again the shadow on the wall leap to an awful life before the light.

The next morning at breakfast Henry Glynn announced that he had to go to the city for three days. The sisters looked at him with surprise. He very seldom left home, and just now his practice had been neglected on account of Edward's death.

'How can you leave your patients now?' asked Mrs Brigham wonderingly.

'I don't know how to, but there is no other way,' replied Henry easily. 'I have had a telegram from Dr. Mitford.'

'Consultation?' inquired Mrs Brigham.

'I have a business,' replied Henry.

Doctor Mitford was an old classmate of his who lived in a neighbouring city and who occasionally called upon him in the case of a consultation.

After he had gone, Mrs Brigham said to Caroline that, after all, Henry had not said that he was going to consult with Doctor Mitford, and she thought it very strange.

'Everything is very strange,' said Rebecca with a shudder.

'What do you mean?' inquired Caroline.

'Nothing,' replied Rebecca.

Nobody entered the study that day, or the next. On the third day, Henry was expected home, but he did not arrive and the last train from the city had come.

'I call it pretty queer work,' said Mrs Brigham. 'The idea of a doctor leaving his patients at such a time as this, and the idea of a consultation lasting three days! There is no sense in it, and now he has not come. I don't understand it, for my part.'

'I don't either,' said Rebecca.

They were all in the south parlour. There was no light in the study; the door was ajar.

Presently Mrs Brigham rose—she could not have told why. Something seemed to impel her—some will outside her own. She went out of the room, again wrapping her rustling skirts around that she might pass noiselessly, and began pushing at the swollen door of the study.

'She has not got any lamp,' said Rebecca in a shaking voice.

Caroline, who was writing letters, rose again, took the only remaining lamp in the room, and followed her sister. Rebecca had risen, but she stood trembling, not venturing to follow.

The doorbell rang, but the others did not hear it. It was on the south door on the other side of the house from the study. Rebecca, after hesitating until the bell rang the second time, went to the door; she remembered that the servant was out.

Caroline and her sister Emma entered the study. Caroline set the lamp on the table. They looked at the wall, and there were two shadows. The sisters stood clutching each other, staring at the awful things on the wall. Then Rebecca came in, staggering, with a telegram in her hand. 'Here is—a telegram,' she gasped. 'Henry is—dead.'

6

Across the Moors

William Fryer Harvey

It really was most unfortunate.

Peggy had a temperature of nearly a hundred, and a pain in her side, and Mrs Workington Bancroft knew that it was appendicitis. But there was no one whom she could send for the doctor.

James had gone with the jaunting car to meet her husband who had at last managed to get away for a week's shooting.

Adolph, she had sent to the Evershams, only half an hour before, with a note for Lady Eva.

The cook could not manage to walk, even if dinner could be served without her.

Kate, as usual, was not to be trusted.

There remained Miss Craig.

'Of course, you must see that Peggy is really ill,' said she, as the governess came into the room, in answer to her summons. 'The difficulty is, that there is absolutely no one whom I can send for the doctor.' Mrs Workington Bancroft paused; she was always willing that those beneath her should have the privilege of offering the services which it was her right to command.

'So, perhaps, Miss Craig,' she went on, 'you would not mind walking over to Tebbits' Farm. I hear there is a Liverpool doctor staying there. Of course, I know nothing about him, but we must take the risk, and I expect he'll be only too glad to be earning something during his holiday. It's nearly four miles, I know, and I'd never dream of asking you if it was not that I dread appendicitis so.'

'Very well,' said Miss Craig, 'I suppose I must go. But I don't know the way.'

'Oh, you can't miss it,' said Mrs Workington Bancroft, in her anxiety temporarily forgiving the obvious unwillingness of her governess' consent.

'You follow the road across the moor for two miles until you come to Redman's Cross. You turn to the left there and follow a rough path that leads through a larch plantation. And Tebbits' farm lies just below you in the valley.'

'And take Pontiff with you,' she added, as the girl left the room. 'There's absolutely nothing to be afraid of, but I expect you'll feel happier with the dog.'

'Well, miss,' said the cook, when Miss Craig went into the kitchen to get her boots, which had been drying by the fire, 'of course she knows best, but I don't think it's right after all that's happened for the mistress to send you across the moors on a night like this. It's not as if the doctor could do anything for Miss Margaret if you do bring him. Every child is like that once in a while. He'll only say put her to bed, and she's there already.'

'I don't see what there is to be afraid of, cook,' said Miss Craig as she laced her boots, 'unless you believe in ghosts.'

'I'm not so sure about that. Anyhow I don't like sleeping in a bed where the sheets are too short for you to pull them over your head. But don't you be frightened, miss. It's my belief that their bark is worse than their bite.'

But though Miss Craig amused herself for some minutes by trying to imagine the bark of a ghost (a thing altogether different from the classical ghostly bark), she did not feel entirely at ease.

She was naturally nervous, and living as she did in the hinterland of the servants' hall, she had heard vague details of true stories that were only myths in the drawing room.

The very name of Redman's Cross sent a shiver through her; it must have been the place where that horrid murder was committed. She had forgotten the tale, though she remembered the name.

Her first disaster came soon enough.

Pontiff, who was naturally slow-witted, took more than five minutes to find out that it was only the governess he was escorting, but once the discovery had been made, he promptly turned tail, paying not the slightest heed to Miss Craig's feeble whistle. And then, to add to her discomfort, the rain came, not in heavy drops, but driving in sheets of thin spray that blotted out what few landmarks there were upon the moor.

They were very kind at Tebbits' farm. The doctor had gone back to Liverpool the day before, but Mrs Tebbit gave her hot milk and turf cakes and offered her reluctant son to show Miss Craig a shorter path on to the moor, that avoided the larch wood.

He was a monosyllabic youth, but his presence was cheering, and she felt the night doubly black when he left her at the last gate.

She trudged on wearily. Her thoughts had already gone back to the almost exhausted theme of the bark of ghosts, when she heard steps on the road behind her that were at least material. Next minute the figure of a man appeared: Miss Craig was relieved to see that the stranger was a clergyman. He raised his hat. 'I believe we are both going in the same direction,' he said.

'Perhaps I may have the pleasure of escorting you.' She thanked him. 'It is rather weird at night,' she went on, 'and what with all the tales of ghosts and bogies that one hears from the country people, I've ended by being half afraid myself.'

'I can understand your nervousness,' he said, 'especially on a night like this. I used at one time to feel the same, for my work often meant lonely walks across the moor to farms which were only reached by rough tracks difficult enough to find even in the daytime.'

'And you never saw anything to frighten you— nothing immaterial I mean?' She asked.

'I can't really say that I did, but I had an experience eleven years ago which served as the turning point in my life, and since you seem to be now in much the same state of mind as I was then in, I will tell it you.

'The time of year was late September. I had been over to Westondale to see an old woman who was dying, and then, just as I was about to start on my way home, word came to me of another of my parishioners who had been suddenly taken ill only that morning. It was after seven when at last I started. A farmer saw me on my way, turning back when I reached the moor road.

'The sunset the previous evening had been one of the loveliest I ever remember seeing. The whole vault of heaven had been scattered with flakes of white cloud, tipped with rosy pink like the strewn petals of a full-blown rose.

'But that night all was changed. The sky was an absolutely dull slate colour, except in one corner of the west where a thin rift showed the last saffron tint of the sullen sunset. As I walked, stiff and footsore, my spirits sank. It must have been the marked contrast between the two evenings, the one so lovely, so full of promise (the corn was still out in the fields spoiling for fine weather), the other so gloomy, so sad with all the dead weight of autumn and winter days to come. And then added to this sense of heavy depression came another different feeling which I surprised myself by recognising as fear.

'I did not know why I was afraid.

'The moors lay on either side of me, unbroken except for a straggling line of turf shooting butts, that stood within a stone's-throw of the road.

'The only sound I had heard for the last half hour was the cry of the startled grouse—Go back, go back, go back. But yet the feeling of fear was there, affecting a low centre of my brain through some little-used physical channel.

'I buttoned my coat closer and tried to divert my thoughts by thinking of next Sunday's sermon.

'I had chosen to preach on Job. There is much in the old-fashioned notion of the book, apart from all the subtleties of the higher criticism, that appeals to country people; the loss of herds and crops, the breakup of the family. I would not have dared to speak, had not I too been a farmer; my own glebe land had been flooded three weeks before, and I suppose I stood to lose as much as any man in the parish. As I walked along the road repeating to myself the first chapter of the book, I stopped at the twelfth verse.

'*And the Lord said unto Satan: Behold all that he hath is in thy power ...*

'The thought of the bad harvest (and that is an awful thought in these valleys) vanished. I seemed to gaze into an ocean of infinite darkness.

'I had often used, with the Sunday glibness of the tired priest, whose duty it is to preach three sermons in one day, the old simile of the chess board. God and the Devil were the players: and we were helping one side or the other. But until that night I had not thought of the possibility of my being only a pawn in the game that God might throw away that the game might be won.

'I had reached the place where we are now, I remember it by that rough stone water-trough, when a man suddenly jumped up from the roadside. He had been seated on a heap of broken road metal.'

'"Which way are you going, guv'ner?" he asked.

'I knew from the way he spoke that the man was a stranger. There are many at this time of the year who come up from the south, tramping northwards with the ripening corn. I told him my destination.

'"We'll go along together," he replied.

'It was too dark to see much of the man's face, but what little I made out was coarse and brutal.

'Then he began the half-menacing whine I knew so well—he had tramped miles that day, he had had no food since breakfast, and that was only a crust.'

'"Give us a copper", he said, "it's only for a night's lodging."

'He was whittling away with a big clasp knife at an ash stake he had taken from some hedge.'

The clergyman broke off.

'Are those the lights of your house?' he said. 'We are nearer than I expected, but I shall have time to finish my story. I think I will, for you can run home in a couple of minutes, and I don't want you to be frightened when you are out on the moors again.

'As the man talked, he seemed to have stepped out of the very background of my thoughts, his sordid tale, with the sad lies that hid a far sadder truth.

'He asked me the time.

'It was five minutes to nine. As I replaced my watch I glanced at his face. His teeth were clenched, and there was something in the gleam of his eyes that told me at once his purpose.

'Have you ever known how long a second is? For a third of a second, I stood there facing him, filled with an overwhelming pity for myself and him, and then without a word of warning, he was upon me. I felt nothing. A flash of lightning ran down my spine, I heard the dull crash of the ash stake, and then a very gentle patter like the sound of a far-distant stream. For a minute I lay in perfect happiness watching the lights of the house as they increased in number until the whole heaven shone with twinkling lamps.

'I could not have had a more painless death.'

Miss Craig looked up. The man was gone. She was alone on the moor.

She ran to the house, her teeth chattering. She ran to the solid shadow that crossed and recrossed the kitchen blind.

As she entered the hall, the clock on the stairs struck the hour. It was nine o'clock.

A Ghost Child

Bernard Capes

In making this confession public, I am aware that I am giving a butterfly to be broken on a wheel. There is so much delicacy in its subject, that the mere resolve to handle it at all might seem to imply a lack of the sensitiveness necessary to its understanding; and it is certain that the more reverent the touch, the more irresistible will figure its opportunity to the common scepticism which is bondslave to its five senses. Moreover, one cannot, in the reason of things, write to publish for Aristarchus alone; but the gauntlet of Grub Street must be run in any bid for truth and sincerity.

On the other hand, to withhold from evidence, in these days of what one may call zetetic psychology, anything which may appear elucidatory—however exquisitely and rarely—of our spiritual relationships, must be pronounced, I think, a sin against the Holy Ghost.

All in all, therefore, I decide to give, with every passage to personal identification safeguarded, the story of a possession or visitation, which is signified in the title of my narrative.

Tryphena was the sole orphaned representative of an obscure but gentle family which had lived for generations in the east of England. The spirit of the fens, of the long grey marshes, whose shores are the neutral ground of two elements, slumbered in her eyes. Looking into them, one seemed to see little beds of tiny green mosses luminous underwater or stirred by the movement of microscopic life in their midst. Secrets, one felt, were shadowed in their depths, too frail and sweet for understanding. The pretty love-fancy of babies seen in the eyes of maidens, was in hers to be interpreted into the very cosmic dust of sea urchins, sparkling like chrysoberyls. Her soul looked out through them, as if they were the windows of a water-nursery.

She was always a child among children, in heart and knowledge most innocent, until Jason came and stood in her field of vision. Then spirit of the neutral ground as she was, inclining to earth or water with the sway of the tides, she came wondering and dripping, as it were, to land, and took up her abode for final choice among the daughters of the earth. She knew her woman's estate, in fact, and the irresistible attraction of all completed perfections to the light that burns to destroy them.

Tryphena was not only an orphan, but an heiress. Her considerable estate was administered by her guardian, Jason's father, a widower, who was possessed of this single adored child. The fruits of parental infatuation had come early to ripen on the seedling. The boy was self-willed and perverse, the more so as he was naturally of a hot-hearted disposition. Violence and remorse would sway him in alternate moods, and be made, each in its turn, a self-indulgence. He took a delight in crossing his father's wishes, and no less in atoning for his gracelessness with moving demonstrations of affection.

Foremost of the old man's most cherished projects was, very naturally, a union between the two young people. He planned, manoeuvred and spoke for it with all his heart of love and eloquence.

And, indeed, it seemed at last as if his hopes were to be crowned. Jason, returning from a lengthy voyage (for his enterprising spirit had early decided for the sea, and he was a naval officer), saw, and was struck amazed before, the transformed vision of his old child-play-fellow. She was an opened flower whom he had left a green bud—a thing so rare and flawless that it seemed a sacrilege for earthly passions to converse of her. Familiarity, however, and some sense of reciprocal attraction, quickly dethroned that eucharist. Tryphena could blush, could thrill, could solicit, in the sweet ways of innocent womanhood. She loved him dearly, wholly, it was plain—had found the realisation of her old formless dreams in this wondrous birth of a desire for one, in whose new-impassioned eves she had known herself reflected hitherto only for the most patronised of small gossips. And, for her part, fearless as nature, she made no secret of her love.

She was absorbed in, a captive to, Jason from that moment and forever.

He responded. What man, however perverse, could have resisted, on first appeal, the attraction of such beauty, the flower of a radiant soul? The two were betrothed; the old man's cup of happiness was brimmed.

Then came clouds and a cold wind, chilling the garden of Hesperis. Jason was always one of those who, possessing classic noses, will cut them off, on easy provocation, to spite their faces.

He was so proudly independent, to himself, that he resented the least assumption of proprietorship in him on the part of other people—even of those who had the best claim to his love and submission. This pride was an obsession. It stultified the real good in him, which was considerable. Apart from it, he was a good, warm-tempered fellow, hasty but affectionate. Under its dominion, he would have broken his own heart on an imaginary grievance.

He found one, it is to be supposed, in the privileges assumed by love; in its exacting claims upon him; perhaps in its little unreasoning jealousies. He distorted these into an implied conceit of authority over him on the part of an heiress who was condescending to his meaner fortunes.

The suggestion was quite base and without warrant; but pride has no balance. No doubt, moreover, the rather childish self-depreciations of the old man, his father, in his attitude towards a match he had so fondly desired, helped to aggravate this feeling. The upshot was that, when within a few months of the date which was to make his union with Tryphena eternal, Jason broke away from a restraint which his pride pictured to him as intolerable, and went on a yachting expedition with a friend.

Then, at once, and with characteristic violence, came the reaction. He wrote, impetuously, frenziedly, from a distant port, claiming himself Tryphena's, and Tryphena to be his, forever and ever and ever. They were man and wife before God. He had behaved like an insensate brute, and he was at that moment starting to speed to her side, to beg her forgiveness and the return of her love.

He had no need to play the suitor afresh. She had never doubted or questioned their mutual bondage, and would have died a maid for his sake. Something of sweet exultation only seemed to quicken and leap in her body, that her faith in her dear love was vindicated.

But the joy came near to upset the reason of the old man, already tottering to its dotage; and what followed destroyed it utterly.

The yacht, flying home, was lost at sea, and Jason was drowned.

I once saw Tryphena about this time. She lived with her near mindless charge, lonely, in an old grey house upon the borders of a salt mere, and had little but the unearthly cries of seabirds to answer to the questions of her widowed heart. She worked, sweet in charity, among the marsh folk, a beautiful unearthly presence; and was especially to be found where infants and the troubles of child-bearing women called for her help and sympathy. She was a wife herself, she would say quaintly; and someday perhaps, by grace of the good spirits of the sea, would be a mother. None thought to cross her statement, put with so sweet a sanity; and, indeed, I have often noticed that the neighbourhood of great waters breeds in souls a mysticism which is remote from the very understanding of land-dwellers.

How I saw her was thus: I was fishing, on a day of chill calm, in a dinghy off the flat coast.

The stillness of the morning had tempted me some distance from the village where I was staying. Presently a sense of bad sport and healthy famine "plumped' in me, so to speak, for luncheon, and I looked about for a spot picturesque enough to add a zest to sandwiches, whisky, and tobacco. Close by, a little creek or estuary ran up into a mere, between which and the sea lay a cluster of low sand-hills; and thither I pulled. The spot, when I reached it, was calm, chill desolation manifest— lifeless water and lifeless sand, with no traffic between them but the dead interchange of salt. Low sedges, at first, and behind them low woods were mirrored in the water at a distance, with an interval between me and them of sheeted glass; and right across this shining pool ran a dim, half-drowned causeway—the sea path, it appeared, to and from a lonely house which I could just distinguish squatting among trees. It was Tryphena's house.

Now, paddling dispiritedly, I turned a cold dune, and saw a mermaid before me. At least, that was my instant impression. The creature sat coiled on the strand, combing her hair—that was certain, for I saw the gold-green tresses of it whisked by her action into rainbow threads. It appeared as certain that her upper half was flesh and her lower fish; and it was only on my nearer approach that this latter resolved itself into a pale green skirt, roped, owing to her posture, about her limbs, and the hem fanned out at her feet into a tail fin. Thus also her bosom, which had appeared naked, became a bodice, as near to her flesh in colour and texture as a smock is to a lady's smock, which some call a cuckoo-flower.

It was plain enough now; yet the illusion for the moment had quite startled me.

As I came near, she paused in her strange business to canvass me. It was Tryphena herself, as after-inquiry informed me. I have never seen so lovely a creature. Her eyes, as they regarded me passing, were something to haunt a dream: so great in tragedy—not fathomless, but all in motion near their surfaces, it seemed, with green and rooted sorrows. They were the eyes, I thought, of an Undine late-humanised, late awakened to the rapturous and troubled knowledge of the woman's burden. Her forehead was most fair, and the glistening thatch divided on it like a golden cloud revealing the face of a wondering angel.

I passed, and a sand-heap stole my vision foot by foot. The vision was gone when I returned. I have reason to believe it was vouchsafed me within a few months of the coming of the ghost-child.

On the morning succeeding the night of the day on which Jason and Tryphena were to have been married, the girl came down from her bedroom with an extraordinary expression of still rapture on her face. After breakfast she took the old man into her confidence. She was childish still; her manner quite youthfully thrilling; but now there was a newborn wonder in it that hovered on the pink of shame.

'Father! I have been under the deep waters and found him. He came to me last night in my dreams—so sobbing, so impassioned—to assure me that he had never really ceased to love me, though he had near broken his own heart pretending it. Poor boy! poor ghost! What could I do but take him in my arms? And all night he lay there, blessed and forgiven, till in the morning he melted away with a sigh that woke me; and it seemed to me that I came up dripping from the sea.'.

'My boy! He has come back!' chuckled the old man. 'What have you done with him, Tryphena?'.

'I will hold him tighter the next time,' she said.

But the spirit of Jason visited her dreams no more.

That was in March. In the Christmas following, when the mere was locked in stillness and the waning reflection of snow mingled on the ceiling with the red dance of firelight, one morning the old man came hurrying and panting to Tryphena's door.

'Tryphena! Come down quickly! My boy, my Jason, has come back! It was a lie that they told us about his being lost at sea!'.

Her heart leapt like a candle-flame! What new delusion of the old man's was this? She hurried over her dressing and descended. A garrulous old voice mingled with a childish treble in the breakfast-room. Hardly breathing, she turned the handle of the door and saw Jason before her.

But it was Jason, the prattling babe of her first knowledge; Jason, the flaxen-headed, apple-cheeked cherub of the nursery; Jason, the confiding, the merry, the loving, before pride had come to warp his innocence. She fell on her knees to the child and with a burst of ecstasy caught him to her heart.

She asked no question of the old man as to when or whence this apparition had come, or why he was here. For some reason she dared not. She accepted him as some waif, whom an accidental likeness had made glorious to their hungering hearts. As for the father, he was utterly satisfied and content. He had heard a knock at the door, he said, and had opened it and found this. The child was naked, and his pink, wet body glazed with ice. Yet he seemed insensible to the killing cold. It was Jason—that was enough. There is no date nor time for imbecility. Its phantoms spring from the clash of ancient memories. This was just as actually his child as—more so, in fact, than—the grown young figure which, for all its manhood, had dissolved into the mist of waters. He was more familiar with, more confident of it, after all. It had come back to be unquestioningly dependent on him; and that was most like the real Jason, flesh of his flesh.

'Who are you, darling?' said Tryphena.

'I am Jason,' answered the child.

She wept, and fondled him rapturously.

'And who am I?' she asked. 'If you are Jason, you must know what to call me.'.

'I know,' he said, 'But I mustn't, unless you ask me.'

'I won't,' she answered, with a burst of weeping. 'It is Christmas Day, dearest, when the miracle of a little child was wrought. I will ask you nothing but to stay and bless our desolate home.'

He nodded, laughing.

'I will stay, until you ask me.'

They found some little old robes of the baby Jason, put away in lavender, and dressed him in them. All day he laughed and prattled; yet it was strange that, talk as he might, he never once referred to matters familiar to the childhood of the lost sailor.

In the early afternoon he asked to be taken out—seawards, that was his wish. Tryphena clothed him warmly, and, taking his little hand, led him away. They left the old man sleeping peacefully.

He was never to wake again.

As they crossed the narrow causeway, snow, thick and silent, began to fall. Tryphena was not afraid, for herself or the child. A rapture upheld her; a sense of some compelling happiness, which she knew before long must take shape on her lips.

They reached the seaward dunes—mere ghosts of foothold in that smoke of flakes. The lap of vast waters seemed all around them, hollow and mysterious. The sound flooded Tryphena's ears, drowning her senses. She cried out and stopped.

'Before they go,' she screamed—'before they go, tell me what you were to call me!'. The child sprang a little distance, and stood facing her. Already his lower limbs seemed dissolving in the mists.

'I was to call you "mother"!' he cried, with a smile and toss of his hand.

Even as he spoke, his pretty features wavered and vanished. The snow broke into him, or he became part of it. Where he had been, a gleam of iridescent dust seemed to show one moment before it sank and was extinguished in the falling cloud. Then there was only the snow, heaping an eternal chaos with nothingness.

Tryphena made this confession, on a Christmas Eve night, to one who was a believer in dreams. The next morning, she was seen to cross the causeway, and thereafter was never seen again. But she left the sweetest memory behind her, for human charity, and an elf-life gift of loveliness..

The Ebony Frame

Edith Nesbit

To be rich is a luxurious sensation—more so when you have plumbed the depths of hard-up-ness as a Fleet Street hack, a picker-up of unconsidered pars, a reporter, an unappreciated journalist—all callings utterly inconsistent with one's family feeling and one's direct descent from the Dukes of Picardy.

When my Aunt Dorcas died and left me seven hundred a year and a furnished house in Chelsea, I felt that life had nothing left to offer except immediate possession of the legacy. Even Mildred Mayhew, whom I had hitherto regarded as my life's light, became less luminous. I was not engaged to Mildred, but I lodged with her mother, and I sang duets with Mildred and gave her gloves when it would run to it, which was seldom. She was a dear good girl, and I meant to marry her someday. It is very nice to feel that a good little woman is thinking of you— it helps you in your work—and it is pleasant to know she will say 'Yes' when you say 'Will you?'

But, as I say, my legacy almost put Mildred out of my head, especially as she was staying with friends in the country just then.

Before the first gloss was off my new mourning I was seated in my aunt's own armchair in front of the fire in the dining-room of my own house. My own house! It was grand but rather lonely. I did think of Mildred just then.

The room was comfortably furnished with oak and leather. On the walls hung a few fairly good oil paintings, but the space above the mantelpiece was disfigured by an exceedingly bad print, 'The Trial of Lord William Russell', framed in a dark frame. I got up to look at it. I had visited my aunt with dutiful regularity, but I never remembered seeing this frame before. It was not intended for a print but for an oil painting. It was of fine ebony, beautifully and curiously carved.

I looked at it with growing interest, and when my aunt's housemaid—I had retained her modest staff of servants—came in with the lamp, I asked her how long the print had been there.

'Mistress only bought it two days afore she took ill,' she said, 'but the frame—she didn't want to buy a new one—so she got this out of the attic. There's lots of curious old things there, sir.'

'Had my aunt had this frame long?'

'Oh yes, sir. It came long afore I did, and I've been here seven years come Christmas. There was a picture in it—that's upstairs too—but it's that black and ugly it might as well be a chimney-back.'

I felt a desire to see this picture. What if it were some priceless old master in which my aunt's eyes had only seen rubbish?

Directly after breakfast the next morning I paid a visit to the lumber room.

It was crammed with old furniture enough to stock a curiosity shop. All the house was furnished solidly in the early Victorian style, and in this room, everything not in keeping with the 'drawing-room suite' ideal was stowed away. Tables of papier mâché and mother-of-pearl, straight-backed chairs with twisted feet and faded needlework cushions, fire screens of old-world design, oak bureau with brass handles, a little work table with its faded, moth-eaten silk flutings hanging in disconsolate shreds; on these and the dust that covered them blazed the full daylight as I drew up the blinds. I promised myself a good time in re-enshrining these household gods in my parlour and promoting the Victorian suite to the attic. But at present my business was to find the picture as 'black as the chimney-back';

and presently, behind a heap of hideous still-life studies, I found it.

Jane the housemaid identified it at once. I took it downstairs carefully and examined it. No subject and no colour were distinguishable. There was a splodge of a darker tint in the middle, but whether it was a figure or tree or house no man could have told. It seemed to be painted on a very thick panel bound with leather. I decided to send it to one of those persons who pour on rotting family portraits the water of eternal youth—mere soap and water Mr Besant tells us it is. But, even as I did so, the thought occurred to me to try my own restorative hand at a corner of it.

My bath sponge, soap and nailbrush vigorously applied for a few seconds showed me that there was no picture to clean! Bare oak presented itself to my persevering brush. I tried the other side, Jane watching me with indulgent interest. The same result. Then the truth dawned on me. Why was the panel so thick? I tore off the leather binding, and the panel divided and fell to the ground in a cloud of dust. There were two pictures—they had been nailed face to face. I leaned them against the wall and the next moment I was leaning against it myself.

For one of the pictures was myself—a perfect portrait—no shade of expression or turn of feature wanting. Myself—in a cavalier dress, 'love locks and all!' When had this been done? And how, without my knowledge?

Was this some whim of my aunt's?

'Lor', sir!' the shrill surprise of Jane at my elbow. 'What a lovely photo it is! Was it a fancy ball, sir?'

'Yes,' I stammered. 'I ... I don't think I want anything more now. You can go.'

She went; and I turned, still with my heart beating violently, to the other picture. This was a woman of the type of beauty beloved of Burne-Jones and Rossetti—straight nose, low brows, full lips, thin hands, large deep luminous eyes. She wore a black velvet gown. It was a full-length portrait. Her arms rested on a table beside her and her head on her hands. But her face was turned full forward and her eyes met those of the spectator bewilderingly.

On the table by her were compasses and instruments whose uses I did not know, books, a goblet, and a miscellaneous heap of papers and pens. I saw all this afterwards. I believe it was a quarter of an hour before I could turn my eyes away from hers. I have never seen any other eyes like hers. They appealed, as a child's or a dog's do; they commanded, as might those of an empress.

'Shall I sweep up the dust, sir?' Curiosity had brought Jane back. I acceded. I turned from her my portrait. I kept between her and the woman in the black velvet. When I was alone again, I tore down 'The Trial of Lord William Russell', and I put the picture of the woman in its strong ebony frame.

Then I wrote to a frame-maker for a frame for my portrait. It had so long-lived face to face with this beautiful witch that I had not the heart to banish it from her presence; from which it will be perceived that I am by nature a somewhat sentimental person.

The new frame came home, and I hung it opposite the fireplace. An exhaustive search among my aunt's papers showed no explanation of the portrait of myself, no history of the portrait of the woman with the wonderful eyes. I only learned that all the old furniture together had come to my aunt at the death of my great-uncle, the head of the family; and I should have concluded that the resemblance was only a family one, if everyone who came in had not exclaimed at the 'speaking likeness'. I adopted Jane's 'fancy ball' explanation.

And there, one might suppose, the matter of the portraits ended. One might suppose it, that is, if there wasn't evidently a good deal more written about it here. However, to me, then, the matter seemed ended.

I went to see Mildred; I invited her and her mother to come and stay with me; I rather avoided glancing at the picture in the ebony frame: I could not forget, nor remember without singular emotion, the look in the eyes of that woman when mine first met them. I shrank from meeting that look again. I reorganised the house somewhat, preparing for Mildred's visit. I turned the dining-room into a drawing room. I brought down much of the old-fashioned furniture, and, after a long day of arranging and re-arranging, I sat down before the fire, and, lying back in a pleasant languor, I idly raised my eyes to the picture. I met her dark, deep, hazel eyes, and once more my gaze was held fixed as by a strong magic—the kind of fascination that keeps one sometimes staring for whole minutes into one's own eyes in the glass. I gazed into her eyes and felt my own dilate, pricked with a smart like the smart of tears.

'I wish,' I said, 'oh, how I wish you were a woman and not a picture!

Come down! Ah, come down!'

I laughed at myself as I spoke. But even as I laughed, I held out my arms.

I was not sleepy. I was not drunk. I was as wide awake and as sober as ever was a man in this world. And yet, as I held out my arms, I saw the eyes of the picture dilate, her lips tremble—if I were to be hanged for saying it, it is true. Her hands moved slightly; and a sort of flicker of a smile passed over her face.

I sprang to my feet. 'This won't do,' I said, still aloud. 'Firelight does play strange tricks. I'll have the lamp.'

I pulled myself together and made for the bell. My hand was on it, when I heard a sound behind me, and turned—the bell still unrung. The fire had burned low, and the corners of the room were deeply shadowed; but, surely, there—behind the tall worked chair—was something darker than a shadow.

'I must face this out,' I said, 'or I shall never be able to face myself again.' I left the bell, I seized the poker, and battered the dull coals to a blaze. Then I stepped back resolutely, and looked up at the picture. The ebony frame was empty! From the shadow of the worked chair came a silken rustle, and out of the shadow the woman of the picture was coming—coming towards me.

I hope I shall never again know a moment of terror so blank and absolute. I could not have moved or spoken to save my life. Either all the known laws of nature were nothing, or I was mad. I stood trembling, but I am thankful to remember, I stood still, while the black velvet gown swept across the hearthrug towards me.

The next moment a hand touched me—a hand soft, warm, and human—and a low voice said, 'You called me. I am here.'

At that touch and that voice, the world seemed to give a sort of bewildering half-turn. I hardly know how to express it, but at once it seemed not awful—not even unusual—for portraits to become flesh—only most natural, most right, most unspeakably fortunate.

I laid my hand on hers. I looked from her to my portrait. I could not see it in the firelight.

'We are not strangers,' I said.

'Oh no, not strangers.' Those luminous eyes were looking up into mine—those red lips were near me. With a passionate cry—a sense of having suddenly recovered life's one great good, that had seemed wholly lost—I clasped her in my arms. She was no ghost—she was a woman—the only woman in the world.

'How long,' I said, 'O love—how long since I lost you?'

She leaned back, hanging her full weight on the hands that were clasped behind my head.

'How can I tell how long? There is no time in hell,' she answered.

It was not a dream. Ah, no—there are no such dreams. I wish to God there could be. When in dreams do I see her eyes, hear her voice, feel her lips against my cheek, hold her hands to my lips, as I did that night— the supreme night of my life? At first, we hardly spoke. It seemed enough ... after long grief and pain ... to feel the arms of my true love.

Round me once again.

It is very difficult to tell this story. There are no words to express the sense of glad reunion, the complete realisation of every hope and dream of a life, that came upon me as I sat with my hand in hers and looked into her eyes.

How could it have been a dream, when I left her sitting in the straight-backed chair and went down to the kitchen to tell the maids I should want nothing more—that I was busy and did not wish to be disturbed? When I fetched wood for the fire with my own hands and, bringing it in, found her still sitting there—saw the little brown head turn as I entered, saw the love in her dear eyes? Or when I threw myself at her feet and blessed the day I was born, since life had given me this?

Not a thought of Mildred. All other things in my life were a dream—this, its one splendid reality.

'I am wondering,' she said after a while, when we had made such cheer each of the other as true lovers may after long parting—'I am wondering how much you remember of our past.'

'I remember nothing,' I said. 'Oh, my dear lady, my dear sweetheart—I remember nothing but that I love you—that I have loved you all my life.'

'You remember nothing—really nothing?'

'Only that I am yours. That we have both suffered. That—tell me, my mistress dear, all that you remember. Explain it all to me. Make me understand. And yet—no, I don't want to understand. It is enough that we are together.'

If it was a dream, why have I never dreamed it again?

She leaned down towards me, her arm lay on my neck, and drew my head till it rested on her shoulder. 'I am a ghost, I suppose,' she said, laughing softly; and her laughter stirred memories which I just grasped at, and just missed. 'But you and I know better, don't we? I will tell you everything you have forgotten. We loved each other—ah! No, you have not forgotten that— and when you came back from the war we were to be married. Our pictures were painted before you went away. You know I was more learned than women of that day. Dear one, when you were gone, they said I was a witch.

They tried me. They said I should be burned. Just because I had looked at the stars and had gained more knowledge than they, they must've wanted to bind me to a stake and let me be eaten by the fire. And you far away!'

Her whole body trembled and shrank. Oh love, what dream would have told me that my kisses would soothe even that memory?

'The night before,' she went on, 'the devil did come to me. I was innocent before—you know it, don't you? And even then, my sin was for you—for you—because of the exceeding love I bore you. The devil came, and I sold my soul to eternal flame. But I got a good price. I got the right to come back, through my picture (if anyone looking at it wished for me), as long as my picture stayed in its ebony frame. That frame was not carved by man's hand. I got the right to come back to you. Oh, my heart's heart, and another thing I won, which you shall hear anon. They burned me for a witch, they made me suffer hell on earth. Those faces, all crowding round, the crackling wood and the smell of the smoke.'

'Oh, love! No more—no more.'

'When my mother sat that night before my picture she wept, and cried, "Come back, my poor lost child!"

And I went to her, with glad leaps of heart.

'Dear, she shrank from me, she fled, she shrieked and moaned of ghosts. She had our pictures covered from sight and put again in the ebony frame. She had promised me my picture should stay always there. Ah, through all these years your face was against mine.'

She paused.

'But the man you loved?'

'You came home. My picture was gone. They lied to you, and you married another woman; but someday I knew you would walk the world again and that I should find you.'

'The other gain?' I asked.

'The other gain,' she said slowly, 'I gave my soul for. It is this. If you also will give up your hopes of heaven I can remain a woman, I can move in your world—I can be your wife. Oh, my dear, after all these years, at last—at last.'

'If I sacrifice my soul,' I said slowly, with no thought of the imbecility of such talk in our 'so-called nineteenth century'—'if I sacrifice my soul, I win you? Why, love, it's a contradiction in terms. You are my soul.'

Her eyes looked straight into mine. Whatever might happen, whatever did happen, whatever may happen, our two souls in that moment met, and became one.

'Then you choose—you deliberately choose—to give up your hopes of heaven for me, as I gave up mine for you?'

'I decline,' I said, 'to give up my hope of heaven on any terms. Tell me what I must do, that you and I may make our heaven here—as now, my dear love.'

'I will tell you tomorrow,' she said. 'Be alone here tomorrow night—twelve is ghost's time, isn't it? And then I will come out of the picture and never go back to it. I shall live with you, and die, and be buried, and there will be an end of me. But we shall live first, my heart's heart.'

I laid my head on her knee. A strange drowsiness overcame me. Holding her hand against my cheek, I lost consciousness. When I awoke the grey November dawn was glimmering, ghost-like, through the uncurtained window. My head was pillowed on my arm which rested—I raised my head quickly—ah! Not on my lady's knee, but on the needle-worked cushion of the straight-backed chair. I sprang to my feet. I was stiff with cold and dazed with dreams, but I turned my eyes to the picture. There she sat, my lady grave, my dear love. I held out my arms, but the passionate cry I would have uttered died on my lips. She had said twelve o'clock. Her lightest word was my law. So, I only stood in front of the picture and gazed into those grey-green eyes till tears of passionate happiness filled my own.

'Oh, my dear, my dear, how shall I pass the hours till I hold you again?'

No thought, then, of my whole life's completion and consummation being a dream.

I staggered up to my room, fell across my bed, and slept heavily and dreamlessly. When I awoke it was high noon. Mildred and her mother were coming to lunch.

I remembered, at one shock, Mildred's coming and her existence.

Now, indeed, the dream began.

With a penetrating sense of the futility of any action apart from her, I gave the necessary orders for the reception of my guests. When Mildred and her mother came, I received them with cordiality; but my genial phrases all seemed to be someone else's. My voice sounded like an echo; my heart was elsewhere.

Still, the situation was not intolerable until the hour when afternoon tea was served in the drawing room. Mildred and her mother kept the conversational pot boiling with a profusion of genteel commonplaces, and I bore it, as one can bear mild purgatories when one is in sight of heaven. I looked up at my sweetheart in the ebony frame, and I felt that anything that might happen, any irresponsible imbecility, any bathos of boredom, was nothing, if, after all, she came to me again.

And yet, when Mildred, too, looked at the portrait, and said, 'What a fine lady! One of your flames, Mr Devigne?' I had a sickening sense of impotent irritation, which became absolute torture when Mildred (how could I ever have admired that chocolate-box barmaid style of prettiness?) threw herself into the high-backed chair, covering the needlework with her ridiculous flounces, and added, 'Silence gives consent! Who is it, Mr Devigne? Tell us all about her: I am sure she has a story.'

Poor little Mildred, sitting there smiling, serene in her confidence that her every word charmed me— sitting there with her rather pinched waist, her rather tight boots, her rather vulgar voice—sitting in the chair where my dear lady had sat when she told me her story! I could not bear it.

'Don't sit there,' I said, 'it's not comfortable!'

But the girl would not be warned. With a laugh that set every nerve in my body vibrating with annoyance, she said, 'Oh, dear! Mustn't I even sit in the same chair as your black-velvet woman?'

I looked at the chair in the picture. It was the same. Mildred was sitting in her chair. Then a horrible sense of Mildred's reality came upon me. Was all this a reality? But for a fortunate chance Mildred might have occupied, not only her chair but her place in my life? I rose.

'I hope you won't think me very rude,' I said, 'but I am obliged to go out.'

I forgot what appointment I had. The lie came readily enough.

I faced Mildred's pouts with the hope that she and her mother would not wait dinner for me. I fled. In another minute I was safe, alone, under the chill, cloudy autumn sky—free to think, think, think of my dear lady.

I walked for hours along streets and squares. I lived over again and again every look, word, hand touch and every kiss. I was completely, unspeakably happy.

Mildred was utterly forgotten. My lady of the ebony frame filled my heart soul and spirit.

As I heard eleven booms through the fog, I turned and went home.

When I got to my street, I found a crowd surging through it, a strong red light filling the air.

A house was on fire. Mine.

I elbowed my way through the crowd.

The picture of my lady—that, at least, I could save!

As I sprang up the steps, I saw, as in a dream—yes, all this was really dream-like—I saw Mildred leaning out of the first-floor window, wringing her hands.

'Come back, sir,' cried a fireman, 'we'll get the young lady out right enough.'

But my lady? I went on up the stairs, cracking, smoking, and as hot as hell, to the room where her picture was. Strange to say, I only felt that the picture was a thing we should like to look on through the long glad wedded life that was to be ours. I never thought of it as being one with her.

As I reached the first floor, I felt arms about my neck. The smoke was too thick for me to distinguish features.

'Save me!' a voice whispered. I clasped a figure in my arms, and, with a strange unease, bore it down the shaking stairs and out into safety. It was Mildred. I knew that directly I clasped her.

'Stand back,' cried the crowd.

'Every one's safe,' cried a fireman.

The flames leapt from every window. The sky grew redder and redder. I sprang from the hands that would have held me. I leapt up the steps. I crawled up the stairs. Suddenly the whole horror of the situation came on me.

'As long as my picture remains in the ebony frame.' What if picture and frame perished together?

I fought with the fire and with my own choking inability to fight with it. I pushed on. I must save my picture. I reached the drawing room.

As I sprang in, I saw my lady—I swear it. Through the smoke and the flames, hold out her arms to me—to me—who came too late to save her and to save my own life's joy. I never saw her again.

Before I could reach her or cry out to her, I felt the floor yield beneath my feet, and I fell into the flames below.

How did they save me? What does that matter? They saved me somehow—curse them. Every stick of my aunt's furniture was destroyed. My friends pointed out that, as the furniture was heavily insured, the carelessness of a nightly-studious housemaid had done me no harm.

No harm!

That was how I won and lost my only love.

I deny, with all my soul in the denial, that it was a dream. There are no such dreams. Dreams of longing and pain there are in plenty, but dreams of complete, of unspeakable happiness—ah, no—it is the rest of life that is the dream.

But if I think that, why have I married Mildred and grown stout and dull and prosperous?

I tell you it is all this that is the dream. My dear lady only is the reality.

And what does it matter what one does in a dream?

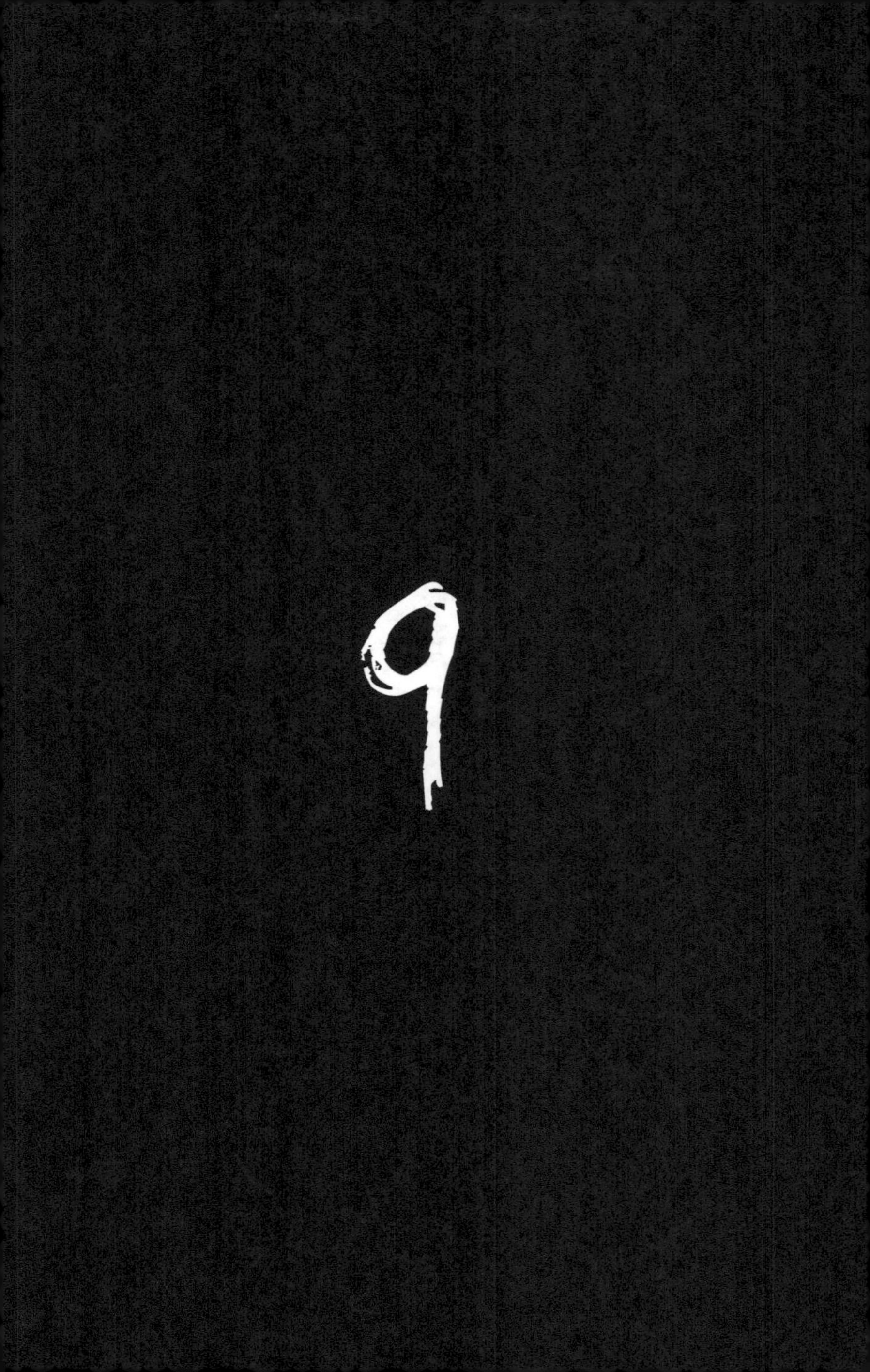
9

The Phantom Coach

Amelia Edwards

The circumstances I am about to relate to you have truth to recommend them. They happened to myself, and my recollection of them is as vivid as if they had taken place only yesterday. Twenty years, however, have gone by since that night. During those twenty years, I have told the story to but one other person. I tell it now with a reluctance that I find difficult to overcome. All I entreat, meanwhile, is that you will abstain from forcing your own conclusions upon me. I want nothing explained away. I desire no arguments. My mind on this subject is quite made up, and, having the testimony of my own senses to rely upon, I prefer to abide by it.

Well! It was just twenty years ago and within a day or two of the end of the grouse season. I had been out all day with my gun and had had no sport to speak of. The wind was due east; the month, December; the place, a bleak wide moor in the far north of England.

And I had lost my way. It was not a pleasant place in which to lose one's way, with the first feathery flakes of a coming snowstorm just fluttering down upon the heather, and the leaden evening closing in all around. I shaded my eyes with my hand and stared anxiously into the gathering darkness, where the purple moorland melted into a range of low hills, some ten or twelve miles distant. Not the faintest smoke wreath, not the tiniest cultivated patch, or fence, or sheep-track, met my eyes in any direction. There was nothing for it but to walk on and take my chance of finding what shelter I could, by the way. So, I shouldered my gun again and pushed wearily forward. For I had been on foot since an hour after daybreak and had eaten nothing since breakfast.

Meanwhile, the snow began to come down with ominous steadiness and the wind fell. After this, the cold became more intense and the night came rapidly up. As for me, my prospects darkened with the darkening sky and my heart grew heavy as I thought how my young wife was already watching for me through the window of our little inn parlour. I thought of all the suffering in store for her throughout this weary night. We had been married four months and having spent our autumn in the Highlands, were now lodging in a remote little village situated just on the verge of the great English moorlands. We were very much in love, and, of course, very happy. This morning, when we parted, she had implored me to return before dusk, and I had promised her that I would. What would I not have given to have kept my word?

Even now, weary as I was, I felt that with a supper, an hour's rest and a guide, I might still get back to her before midnight, if only guide and shelter could be found.

And all this time, the snow fell and the night thickened. I stopped and shouted now and then, but my shouts seemed only to make the silence deeper. Then a vague sense of uneasiness came upon me, and I began to remember stories of travellers who had walked on and on in the falling snow until wearied out, they were fain to lie down and sleep their lives away. Would it be possible, I asked myself, to keep on thus through all the long dark night? Would there not come a time when my limbs must fail, and my resolution give way? When I, too, must sleep the sleep of death. Death! I shuddered. How hard to die just now, when life lay all so bright before me! How hard for my darling, whose whole loving heart but that thought was not to be borne! To banish it, I shouted again, louder and longer, and then listened eagerly. Was my shout answered, or did I only fancy that I heard a far-off cry? I hallooed again, and again the echo followed. Then a wavering speck of light came suddenly out of the dark, shifting, disappearing, growing momentarily nearer and brighter. Running towards it at full speed, I found myself, to my great joy, face to face with an old man and a lantern.

'Thank God!' was the exclamation that burst involuntarily from my lips.

Blinking and frowning, he lifted his lantern and peered into my face.

'What for?' growled he, sulkily.

'Well—for you. I began to fear I should be lost in the snow.'

'Eh, then, folks do get cast away hereabouts fra' time to time, an' what's to hinder you from bein' cast away likewise, if the Lord's so minded?'

'If the Lord is so minded that you and I shall be lost together, friend, we must submit,' I replied; 'but I don't mean to be lost without you. How far am I now from Dwolding?'

'A good twenty mile, more or less.'

'And the nearest village?'

'The nearest village is Wyke, an' that's twelve-mile t'other side.'

'Where do you live, then?'

'Out yonder,' said he, with a vague jerk of the lantern.

'You're going home, I presume?'

'Maybe I am.'

'Then I'm going with you.'

The old man shook his head and rubbed his nose reflectively with the handle of the lantern.

'It ain't o' no use,' growled he. 'He 'ont let you in—not he.'

'We'll see about that,' I replied, briskly. 'Who is He?'

'The master.'

'Who is the master?'

'That's nowt to you,' was the unceremonious reply.

'Well, well! You lead the way and I'll engage that the master shall give me shelter and a supper tonight.'

'Eh, you can try him!' muttered my reluctant guide; and, still shaking his head, he hobbled, gnome-like, away through the falling snow. A large mass loomed up presently out of the darkness, and a huge dog rushed out, barking furiously.

'Is this the house?' I asked.

'Ay, it's the house. Down, Bey!' And he fumbled in his pocket for the key.

I drew up close behind him, prepared to lose no chance of entrance, and saw in the little circle of light shed by the lantern that the door was heavily studded with iron nails, like the door of a prison. In another minute he had turned the key and I had pushed past him into the house.

Once inside, I looked round with curiosity and found myself in a great raftered hall, which served, apparently, a variety of uses. One end was piled to the roof with corn, like a barn. The other was stored with flour sacks, agricultural implements, casks, and all kinds of miscellaneous lumber; while from the beams overhead hung rows of hams, flitches, and bunches of dried herbs for winter use. In the centre of the floor stood some huge object gauntly dressed in a dingy wrapping-cloth, and reaching halfway to the rafters. Lifting a corner of this cloth, I saw, to my surprise, a telescope of very considerable size, mounted on a rude movable platform, with four small wheels. The tube was made of painted wood, bound round with bands of metal rudely fashioned; the speculum, so far as I could estimate its size in the dim light, measured at least fifteen inches in diameter. While I was yet examining the instrument, and asking myself whether it was not the work of some self-taught optician, a bell rang sharply.

'That's for you,' said my guide, with a malicious grin. 'Yonder's his room.'

He pointed to a low black door at the opposite side of the hall. I crossed over, rapped somewhat loudly, and went in, without waiting for an invitation. A huge, white-haired old man rose from a table covered with books and papers and confronted me sternly.

'Who are you?' said he. 'How come you here? What do you want?'

'James Murray, barrister-at-law. On foot across the moor. Meat, drink and sleep.'

He bent his bushy brows into a portentous frown.

'Mine is not a house of entertainment,' he said, haughtily. 'Jacob, how dared you admit this stranger?'

'I didn't admit him,' grumbled the old man. 'He followed me over the moor and shouldered his way in before me. I'm no match for six foot two.'

'And pray, sir! By what right have you forced an entrance into my house?'

'The same by which I should have clung to your boat, if I were drowning. The right of self-preservation.'

'Self-preservation?'

'There's an inch of snow on the ground already,' I replied, briefly; 'and it would be deep enough to cover my body before daybreak.'

He strode to the window, pulled aside a heavy black curtain, and looked out.

'It is true,' he said. 'You can stay, if you choose, till morning. Jacob, serve the supper.'

With this, he waved me to a seat, resumed his own, and became at once absorbed in the studies from which I had disturbed him.

I placed my gun in a corner, drew a chair to the hearth, and examined my quarters at leisure. Smaller and less incongruous in its arrangements than the hall, this room contained, nevertheless, much to awaken my curiosity. The floor was carpetless. The whitewashed walls were in parts scrawled over with strange diagrams, and in others covered with shelves crowded with philosophical instruments, the uses of many of which were unknown to me. On one side of the fireplace, stood a bookcase filled with dingy folios; on the other, a small organ, fantastically decorated with painted carvings of medieval saints and devils. Through the half-opened door of a cupboard at the further end of the room, I saw a long array of geological specimens, surgical preparations, crucibles, retorts, and jars of chemicals; while on the mantelshelf beside me, amid a number of small objects, stood a model of the solar system, a small galvanic battery, and a microscope. Every chair had its burden. Every corner was heaped high with books. The very floor was littered over with maps, casts, papers, tracings, and learned lumber of all conceivable kinds.

I stared about me with an amazement increased by every fresh object upon which my eyes chanced to rest. So strange a room I had never seen; yet seemed it stranger still, to find such a room in a lone farmhouse amid those wild and solitary moors! Over and over again, I looked from my host to his surroundings, and from his surroundings back to my host, asking myself who and what he could be. His head was singularly fine, but it was more the head of a poet than of a philosopher. Broad in the temples, prominent over the eyes, and clothed with a rough profusion of perfectly white hair, it had all the ideality and much of the ruggedness that characterises the head of Louis von Beethoven. There were the same deep lines about the mouth and the same stern furrows in the brow. There was the same concentration of expression. While I was yet observing him, the door opened, and Jacob brought in the supper. His master then closed his book, rose, and with more courtesy of manner than he had yet shown, invited me to the table.

A dish of ham and eggs, a loaf of brown bread, and a bottle of admirable sherry, were placed before me.

'I have but the homeliest farmhouse fare to offer

you, sir,' said my entertainer. 'Your appetite, I trust, will make up for the deficiencies of our larder.'

I had already fallen upon the viands, and now protested, with the enthusiasm of a starving sportsman, that I had never eaten anything so delicious.

He bowed stiffly and sat down to his own supper, which consisted, primitively, of a jug of milk and a basin of porridge. We ate in silence and when we were done Jacob removed the tray. I then drew my chair back to the fireside. My host, somewhat to my surprise, did the same, and turning abruptly towards me, said, 'Sir, I have lived here in strict retirement for three-and-twenty years. During that time, I have not seen as many strange faces, and I have not read a single newspaper. You are the first stranger who has crossed my threshold for more than four years. Will you favour me with a few words of information respecting that outer world from which I have parted company so long?'

'Pray interrogate me,' I replied. 'I am heartily at your service.'

He bent his head in acknowledgment and leaned forward, with his elbows resting on his knees and his chin supported in the palms of his hands. He stared fixedly into the fire and proceeded to question me.

His inquiries related chiefly to scientific matters,

with the later progress of which, as applied to the practical purposes of life, he was almost wholly unacquainted. No student of science myself, I replied as well as my slight information permitted; but the task was far from easy, and I was much relieved when, passing from interrogation to discussion, he began pouring forth his own conclusions upon the facts which I had been attempting to place before him. He talked, and I listened spellbound. He talked till I believe he almost forgot my presence, and only thought aloud. I had never heard anything like it then; I have never heard anything like it since. Familiar with all systems of all philosophies, subtle in analysis, bold in generalisation, he poured forth his thoughts in an uninterrupted stream, and, still leaning forward in the same moody attitude with his eyes fixed upon the fire, wandered from topic to topic, from speculation to speculation, like an inspired dreamer. From practical science to mental philosophy; from electricity in the wire to electricity in the nerve; from Watts to Mesmer, from Mesmer to Reichenbach, from Reichenbach to Swedenborg, Spinoza, Condillac, Descartes, Berkeley, Aristotle, Plato, and the Magi and mystics of the East, were transitions which, however bewildering in their variety and scope, seemed easy and harmonious upon his lips as sequences in music. By and by I forget now by what link of conjecture or illustration—he passed on to that field which lies beyond the boundary line of even conjectural philosophy, and reaches no man knows whither. He spoke of the soul and its aspirations. Of the spirit and its powers. Of second sight, prophecy, of those phenomena which, under the names of ghosts, spectres and supernatural appearances, have been denied by the sceptics and attested by the credulous, of all ages.

'The world,' he said, 'grows hourly more and more sceptical of all that lies beyond its own narrow radius. And our men of science foster the fatal tendency. They condemn as fable all that resists experiment. They reject as false all that cannot be brought to the test of the laboratory or the dissecting room. Against what superstition have they waged so long and obstinate a war, as against the belief in apparitions? And yet what superstition has maintained its hold upon the minds of men so long and so firmly? Show me any fact in physics, in history, in archaeology, which is supported by testimony so wide and so various. Attested by all races of men, in all ages, and all climates, by the soberest sages of antiquity, by the rudest savage of today, by the Christian, the Pagan, the Pantheist, the Materialist, this phenomenon is treated as a nursery tale by the philosophers of our century. Circumstantial evidence weighs with them as a feather in the balance. The comparison of causes with effects, however valuable in physical science, is put aside as worthless and unreliable. The evidence of competent witnesses, however conclusive in a court of justice, counts for nothing. He who pauses before he pronounces is condemned as a trifler. He who believes is a dreamer or a fool.'

He spoke with bitterness, and, having said thus, relapsed for some minutes into silence. Presently he raised his head from his hands, and added, with an altered voice and manner, 'Sir, I paused, investigated, believed and was not ashamed to state my convictions to the world. I, too, was branded as a visionary, held up to ridicule by my contemporaries, and hooted from that field of science in which I had laboured with honour during all the best years of my life. These things happened just three and twenty years ago. Since then, I have lived as you see me living now, and the world has forgotten me, as I have forgotten the world. You have my history.'

'It is a very sad one,' I murmured, scarcely knowing what to answer.

'It is a very common one,' he replied. 'I have only suffered for the truth, as many a better and wiser man has suffered before me.'

He rose, as if desirous of ending the conversation, and went over to the window.

'It has ceased snowing,' he observed, as he dropped the curtain, and came back to the fireside.

'Ceased!' I exclaimed, starting eagerly to my feet. 'Oh, if it were only possible—but no! it is hopeless. Even if I could find my way across the moor, I could not walk twenty miles tonight.'

'Walk twenty miles tonight!' repeated my host. 'What are you thinking of?'

'Of my wife,' I replied, impatiently. 'Of my young wife, who does not know that I have lost my way, and who is at this moment breaking her heart with suspense and terror.'

'Where is she?'

'At Dwolding, twenty miles away.'

'At Dwolding,' he echoed, thoughtfully. 'Yes, the distance, it is true, is twenty miles; but—are you so very anxious to save the next six or eight hours?'

'So very, very anxious, that I would give ten guineas at this moment for a guide and a horse.'

'Your wish can be gratified at a less costly rate,' said he, smiling. 'The night mail from the north, which changes horses at Dwolding, passes within five miles of this spot, and will be due at a certain cross-road in about an hour and a quarter. If Jacob were to go with you across the moor, and put you into the old coach-road, you could find your way, I suppose, to where it joins the new one?'

'Easily—gladly.'

He smiled again, rang the bell, gave the old servant his directions, and, taking a bottle of whisky and a wineglass from the cupboard in which he kept his chemicals, said:

'The snow lies deep, and it will be difficult walking to-night on the moor. A glass of usquebaugh before you start?'

I would have declined the spirit, but he pressed it on me, and I drank it. It went down my throat like liquid flame, and almost took my breath away.

'It is strong,' he said; 'but it will help to keep out the cold. And now you have no moments to spare. Good night!'

I thanked him for his hospitality and would have shaken hands. But that he had turned away before I could finish my sentence. In another minute I had traversed the hall, Jacob had locked the outer door behind me, and we were out on the wide white moor.

Although the wind had fallen, it was still bitterly cold. Not a star glimmered in the black vault overhead. Not a sound, save the rapid crunching of the snow beneath our feet, disturbed the heavy stillness of the night. Jacob, not too well pleased with his mission, shambled on before in sullen silence, his lantern in his hand, and his shadow at his feet. I followed, with my gun over my shoulder, as little inclined for conversation as himself. My thoughts were full of my late host. His voice yet rang in my ears. His eloquence yet held my imagination captive. I remember to this day, with surprise, how my over-excited brain retained whole sentences and parts of sentences, troops of brilliant images, and fragments of splendid reasoning, in the very words in which he had uttered them. Musing thus over what I had heard, and striving to recall a lost link here and there, I strode on at the heels of my guide, absorbed and unobservant. Presently—at the end, as it seemed to me, of only a few minutes—he came to a sudden halt, and said:

'Yon's your road. Keep the stone fence to your right hand and you can't fail of the way.'

'This, then, is the old coach road?'

'Ay, 'tis the old coach-road.'

'And how far do I go, before I reach the cross-roads?'

'Nigh upon three miles.'

I pulled out my purse, and he became more communicative.

'The road's a fair road enough,' said he, 'for foot passengers; but 'twas over steep and narrow for the northern traffic. You'll mind where the parapet's broken away, close again the signpost. It's never been mended since the accident.'

'What accident?'

'Eh, the night mail pitched right over into the valley below—a good fifty feet an' more—just at the worst bit o' road in the whole county.'

'Horrible! Were many lives lost?'

'All. Four were found dead, and t'other two died next morning.'

'How long is it since this happened?'

'Just nine years.'

'Near the signpost, you say? I will bear it in mind. Good night.'

'Gude night, sir, and thankee.' Jacob pocketed his half-crown, made a faint pretence of touching his hat, and trudged back by the way he had come.

I watched the light of his lantern till it quite disappeared, and then turned to pursue my way alone. This was no longer a matter of the slightest difficulty, for, despite the dead darkness overhead, the line of stone fence showed distinctly enough against the pale gleam of the snow. How silent it seemed now, with only my footsteps to listen to; how silent and how solitary! A strange disagreeable sense of loneliness stole over me. I walked faster. I hummed a fragment of a tune. I cast up enormous sums in my head and accumulated them at compound interest. I did my best. In short, to forget the startling speculations to which I had but just been listening, and, to some extent, I succeeded.

Meanwhile, the night air seemed to become colder and colder, and though I walked fast I found it impossible to keep myself warm. My feet were like ice. I lost sensation in my hands and grasped my gun mechanically. I even breathed with difficulty, as though, instead of traversing a quiet north country highway, I were scaling the uppermost heights of some gigantic Alp. This last symptom became presently so distressing, that I was forced to stop for a few minutes and lean against the stone fence. As I did so, I chanced to look back up the road, and there, to my infinite relief, I saw a distant point of light, like the gleam of an approaching lantern. I, at first, concluded that Jacob had retraced his steps and followed me; but even as the conjecture presented itself, a second light flashed into sight—a light parallel with the first, and approaching at the same rate of motion. It needed no second thought to show me that these must be the carriage lamps of some private vehicle, though it seemed strange that any private vehicle should take a road professedly disused and dangerous

There could be no doubt, however, of the fact, for the lamps grew larger and brighter every moment, and I even fancied I could already see the dark outline of the carriage between them. It was coming up very fast, and quite noiselessly, the snow being nearly a foot deep under the wheels.

And now the body of the vehicle became distinctly visible behind the lamps. It looked strangely lofty. A sudden suspicion flashed upon me. Was it possible that I had passed the crossroads in the dark without observing the signpost, and could this be the very coach which I had come to meet?

No need to ask myself that question a second time, for here it came round the bend of the road. The guard and driver, one outside passenger and four steaming greys, all were wrapped in a soft haze of light, through which the lamps blazed out, like a pair of fiery meteors.

I jumped forward, waved my hat, and shouted. The mail came down at full speed and passed me. For a moment I feared that I had not been seen or heard, but it was only for a moment. The coachman pulled up; the guard, muffled to the eyes in capes and comforters, and

apparently sound asleep in the rumble, neither answered my hail nor made the slightest effort to dismount; the outside passenger did not even turn his head. I opened the door for myself and looked in. There were but three travellers inside, so I stepped in, shut the door, slipped into the vacant corner, and congratulated myself on my good fortune.

The atmosphere of the coach seemed, if possible, colder than that of the outer air, and was pervaded by a singularly damp and disagreeable smell. I looked around at my fellow passengers. They were all three, men, and all silent. They did not seem to be asleep, but each leaned back in his corner of the vehicle, as if absorbed in his own reflections. I attempted to open a conversation.

'How intensely cold it is tonight,' I said, addressing my opposite neighbour.

He lifted his head and looked at me, but made no reply.

'The winter,' I added, 'seems to have begun in earnest.'

Although the corner in which he sat was so dim that I could distinguish none of his features very clearly, I saw that his eyes were still turned full upon me. And yet he answered never a word.

At any other time, I should have felt, and perhaps expressed some annoyance, but at the moment I felt too ill to do either. The icy coldness of the night air had struck a chill to my very marrow. And the strange smell inside the coach was affecting me with intolerable nausea. I shivered from head to foot. And, turning to my left-hand neighbour, asked if he had any objection to an open window.

He neither spoke nor stirred.

I repeated the question somewhat more loudly but with the same result. Then I lost patience, and let the sash down. As I did so, the leather strap broke in my hand, and I observed that the glass was covered with a thick coat of mildew, the accumulation, apparently, of years. My attention being thus drawn to the condition of the coach, I examined it more narrowly and saw by the uncertain light of the outer lamps that it was in the last stage of dilapidation. Every part of it was not only out of repair but in a condition of decay. The sashes splintered at a touch. The leather fittings were crusted over with mould and literally rotting from the woodwork. The floor was almost breaking away beneath my feet. The whole machine, in short, was foul with damp and had been dragged from some outhouse in which it had been mouldering away for years, to do another day or two of duty on the road.

I turned to the third passenger, whom I had not yet addressed, and hazarded one more remark.

'This coach,' I said, 'is in a deplorable condition. The regular mail, I suppose, is under repair?'

He moved his head slowly, and looked me in the face, without speaking a word. I shall never forget that look while I live. I turned cold at heart under it. I turn cold at heart even now when I recall it. His eyes glowed with a fiery unnatural lustre. His face was as livid as the face of a corpse. His bloodless lips were drawn back as if in the agony of death and showed the gleaming teeth between.

The words that I was about to utter died upon my lips, and a strange horror—a dreadful horror—came upon me. My sight had by this time become used to the gloom of the coach, and I could see with tolerable distinctness. I turned to my opposite neighbour. He, too, was looking at me, with the same startling pallor in his face, and the same stony glitter in his eyes. I passed my hand across my brow. I turned to the passenger on the seat beside my own, and saw—oh Heaven! How shall I describe what I saw? I saw that he was no living man—that none of them were living men, like myself! A pale phosphorescent light—the light of putrefaction—

played upon their awful faces; upon their hair, dank with the dews of the grave; upon their clothes, earth-stained and dropping to pieces; upon their hands, which were as the hands of corpses long buried. Only their eyes, their terrible eyes, were living; and those eyes were all turned menacingly upon me!

A shriek of terror, a wild unintelligible cry for help and mercy; burst from my lips as I flung myself against the door, and strove in vain to open it.

In that single instant, brief and vivid as a landscape beheld in the flash of summer lightning, I saw the moon shining down through a rift of stormy cloud—the ghastly sign-post rearing its warning finger by the wayside—the broken parapet—the plunging horses—the black gulf below. Then, the coach reeled like a ship at sea. Then, came a mighty crash—a sense of crushing pain—and then, darkness.

It seemed as if years had gone by when I awoke one morning from a deep sleep and found my wife watching by my bedside I will pass over the scene that ensued, and give you, in half a dozen words, the tale she told me with tears of thanksgiving. I had fallen over a precipice, close against the junction of the old coach road and the new, and had only been saved from certain death by lighting upon a deep snowdrift that had accumulated at the foot of the rock beneath. In this snowdrift, I was discovered at daybreak, by a couple of shepherds, who carried me to the nearest shelter and brought a surgeon to my aid. The surgeon found me in a state of raving delirium, with a broken arm and a compound fracture of the skull. The letters in my pocketbook showed my name and address; my wife was summoned to nurse me; and, thanks to youth and a fine constitution, I came out of danger at last. The place of my fall, I need scarcely say, was precisely that at which a frightful accident had happened to the north mail nine years before.

I never told my wife the fearful events which I have just related to you. I told the surgeon who attended me. But he treated the whole adventure as a mere dream born of the fever in my brain. We discussed the question over and over again until we found that we could discuss it with temper no longer, and then we dropped it. Others may form what conclusions they please—I know that twenty years ago I was the fourth inside passenger in that Phantom Coach.

10

Concert to Death

Paul Ernst

The stage was illuminated brightly, rawly. Every ridge on the ugly steel fire curtain stood out in the ghostly white radiance. On the stage were a concert grand piano and a battered piano stool. The top of the piano was down, shutting in the sounding board. A black drape was thrown over it. A vase of yellow roses was set on the closed, draped lid. All was in readiness for Lucchesi to enter from the wings, to bow and smile as he walked to the piano, as he had done so many times in his life. Everything was as the master pianist liked it's his favourite, battered old piano stool; piano set in the right-centre of a perfectly bare stage; nothing but the raw steel fire-curtain for a backdrop; harsh, uncompromising light.

Only the piano itself was different. For it is not usual for the lid of a concert grand to be down during a performance, nor for the case to be draped and to support a vase of flowers or anything else that might muffle pure clarity of tone. In the orchestra pit sat the orchestra, instruments tuned and ready, musical scores opened on the racks before each member, tiny lights glimmering like glow-worms over the racks. The orchestra conductor stood before them with arms poised like the wings of a bird about to take off, and with his head back to nod for the opening crash of harmony. Behind him, in the great auditorium with its thousands of seats, a breathless hush prevailed. In the hush, the gradual dimming of the indirect lights overhead had been like a silent dusk over an unrippled lake. In the vast silence, just one sound was heard, for an instant—a woman's sobbing. The conductor's arms swooped down. The opening bar of Lucchesi's Minuet in G flooded the huge hall with quivering melody. Every instrument was adding to the tide of music—but the piano. Every musician was playing—but the great Lucchesi himself. The sobbing sounded again, instantly stifled. The piece, a short one, drew to its conclusion and silence again held the house. The conductor turned from his rack and faced the thousands of seats. He raised his baton as though to still thunderous applause; which was odd, because there was no applause.

'We will now play Lucchesi's "Dance of the Sprites,"' the conductor said. And his voice rang in the auditorium with the hollow boom of a voice in an empty cavern. Rightly so! For there was no one in the vast hall. The thousands of seats were empty. The boxes, galleries and balconies were empty. On the bare stage was Lucchesi's piano. Yes, but there was no Lucchesi there to play it. There never would be again. Lucchesi was dead.

'Kind of gets you, doesn't it,' whispered one of the three men in the left wing. The three were Howard Kent, star reporter for the Globe, who was here on sufferance and not for publicity purposes; Milnor Roberts, music critic on the same newspaper; and Isaac Loewenbohn, owner of the auditorium. It was Kent who had spoken. 'Kind of gets you,' he repeated, looking across the length of the bare stage between the floodlights and the fire curtain. In the other wing, a woman stood alone. A woman dressed in mourning, with a white face, stood out against the black like a dainty white cameo. The woman's red underlip was caught between her teeth and her body shook with suppressed sobs.

'It's certainly a unique idea,' Kent whispered on. He was afraid that if he didn't talk, he would get sloppy, which is no way for a hardboiled reporter to get. 'Staging a Lucchesi concert when Lucchesi is food for worms. Eccentric idea.'

'A nice idea, I think,' said Loewenbohn, scowling at the reporter. 'Today, one year from the day Lucchesi has died, his friends and fellow musicians hold an all-Lucchesi concert in memoriam. That is a nice tribute.' Roberts, the music critic, nodded abstractedly. His mind was full of the piece the orchestra was now playing. 'Dance of the Sprites' had been written for a piano lead. There were three long interludes in it when only the piano played—and the piano on the stage had no player before its keyboard! 'Wonder how they'll treat the piano interludes,' he whispered to Loewenbohn as the first one drew near. 'Will they fill in?'

The auditorium owner shrugged. There was a piano in the pit. Perhaps the orchestra pianist would play Lucchesi's interludes. But the conductor was more subdued than that. The three men leaned forward a little as the composition reached the first interlude and died away in a shower of flute notes. Now it was time for the piano to pick up the thread. Now it was time for Lucchesi to crash in. . . . Only there was no Lucchesi. There was silence, while the conductor faced the piano on the stage, with his baton at rest by his side. Silence. The tense, oppressive silence that comes when music is interrupted, but when you know the piece is not yet finished. In that silence conductor and orchestra stared at the piano on the stage; stared and held their instruments in readiness to play again. There was an eery matter-of-factness about orchestra and conductor. It was as though of course Lucchesi was seated on the stool; of course, he was playing his piano. Death? They were wordlessly realising its power. Particularly the conductor ...

'Look at him!' muttered the reporter, running his forefinger around under his collar. 'Look at him!' The orchestra leader's body was swaying very slightly. His eyes were wide, mystic, as he stared at the piano—and at the empty stool. 'You'd think Lucchesi really was there, playing!' The other two paid no attention to him. The critic softly hummed the interlude Lucchesi would be playing if he were alive. Loewenbohn's heavy face seemed less florid than usual. The critic stopped humming. Even as he did so, the conductor raised his baton and the orchestra went on with the composition, softly, for the piano notes were supposed to sound over the other instruments for a few more bars. Kent moistened his lips and stared at the keyboard. Curious. For just an instant it had seemed to him that the keys were being rhythmically depressed, as though at the touch of unseen fingers. But that, of course, was imagination. The piano standing on the bare stage in lonely majesty.

The funeral drape over the closed case and the scent of the yellow roses; the sombre dignity with which the orchestra played to an empty auditorium. These things tended to make you see what did not exist. 'Marvellous stuff, that music,' Kent said, resolutely keeping the shiver out of his voice. Roberts nodded.

'Lucchesi had supreme genius. It was tragic that he had to die.'

'Yeah. And only forty-one. A guy that could turn out stuff like this!' Roberts smiled.

'Yes, this is superb. But it's not as fine as Lucchesi's last composition—one he finished just before he died last year. That piece was greatest of all.' Loewenbohn's heavy eyebrows went up. 'I don't think I ever heard of that piece,' he said. 'Few have,' replied Roberts. 'And no one ever heard it played. It's lost.'

'Huh!' said Kent. 'But if nobody ever heard it, how do you know it was so great.'

'The critic shrugged. 'Lucchesi said it was,' he said simply. 'He worked on it for nearly a year, in secret, as he always composed. He finished it. He told me and one or two other close friends about it. He died—and no one has ever been able to find the score.' Kent shook his head. 'That's tough. And Mrs. Lucchesi is flat broke, too. I did a story on her six months ago. Living with

her sister —lost the insurance money—even Lucchesi's piano in storage. By the way, the piano on the stage is really Lucchesi's own, isn't it?' Roberts looked at the shrouded piano and nodded. 'We got it out of storage for the occasion. Tomorrow—' he looked across at Lucchesi's widow, '—it is to be sold at auction. She has to have money.'

'If only she could find the song!' sympathised Kent. 'It would mean a lot to her,' responded Roberts. 'There's no real wealth in genius. But the song would bring several thousand dollars. And it would bring Lucchesi tremendous posthumous fame.' He stopped talking. The second piano interlude was heard. The orchestral notes slowed. The conductor and each musician in the pit gazed at the draped piano. Instinctively the three men in the left wing stared at it too. And in the right wing Lucchesi's widow swayed forward a little, with her arms going out and her lips parting. The orchestra stopped playing. Everything was in readiness. All was waiting on Lucchesi, who would play no more. But as the thick stillness of the interlude continued, Kent, watching the keyboard of Lucchesi's piano with eyes that were less cynical than usual, began to have an insane idea that perhaps the great composer was here at the concert held in his memory. Surely there was a tall, shadowy figure seated on the old stool. Surely long, steely fingers were flying over the keyboard. Surely a shower of notes was sounding from the instrument that had known for so long the touch of those fingers.

The conductor was again swaying, as though to a cascade of harmony. But now his eyes were wide, almost frightened-looking; and his mouth was a little open and his head was bent as though he dimly heard something not quite audible to others there. The musicians, too, in this second, almost ghastly silence, were not quite the same as they had been in the first interlude. They were rigid in the pit, the lights over their racks reflecting on the whites of their staring eyes and traces of moisture on their tense faces. Kent drew a deep breath and glanced at Roberts and Loewenbohn quickly to see if they had heard how shaky his sigh was. The atmosphere of this memorial concert—this concert to death had changed. A new element had entered it, somehow. A sort of electricity charged the air. Kent could feel it. He knew the others felt it. He found himself holding his breath. Waiting, waiting … but for what? He did not know. Once more he tore his eyes from the keyboard of Lucchesi's piano. The keys were not moving! How could they, with no fingers to move them.

He saw Lucchesi's widow stagger a little and started impulsively toward her. She raised her slim hand and waved him back. The conductor raised his baton. Sweat was glistening on his forehead. He waved his arms, and the musicians, with an obvious effort, swung into the Dance. Kent gulped with relief as the hushed stillness was broken. The strain was lifted a little now; and he took refuge from his inexplicable nervousness by telling himself that this whole thing was a silly farce: getting Loewenbohn to donate the place this afternoon, scraping up an orchestra, dragging Lucchesi's piano from the warehouse—and then acting as though the dead man were here and playing before an accustomed audience! Crazy! And it was ripping Lucchesi's widow to pieces. He stared across at her and was alarmed by her pallor. They simply shouldn't have permitted this. She must be terribly broke—forced to put Lucchesi's piano in storage because she had no home of her own to put it in. And it must be the devil for her to have to sell it. It would bring a good price, though. Lucchesi's own piano ...

'You say they looked everywhere for that last composition of his?' he whispered to Roberts under cover of the music. The critic nodded. 'Of course. All his effects were gone over.' His voice was like Kent's.

Not quite steady, a little strained. And his eyes, like Kent's, were continually turning toward the keyboard of the draped piano. 'I helped in the search myself. But he'd hidden it too well.'

'Hidden it?' repeated Kent. 'Why did he hide it?' 'He thought somebody was trying to steal it. At the very least, he was not a good man. He had delusions. But there were no delusions about his composition. That must have been grand.' The music welling from the musicians in the pit was sublime. No man there had ever played so well before. They were inspired, playing beyond themselves, as though they themselves were but instruments manipulated by a master hand. The third, and last, piano interlude in 'Dance of the Sprites', drew near. The orchestral notes began fading as the piano was supposed to pick up the thread of the composition. Kent scowled. 'I wish they wouldn't do this! It's … it's … damn it, it's ghostly!' 'Shut up,' whispered Roberts, his voice thin. The last note died away. The great, empty hall swam again in silence. Live, electric silence. Every gaze was riveted on the black-draped piano on the bare stage. Again, the illusion came to Kent, terrifically, that there was a figure on the stool, that long fingers raced over the keyboard in the climactic crash of the interlude.

Surely, surely …. Roberts started and stared first at the piano on the stage and then at the piano in the pit. His mouth hung open and his face paled. The great vein in his throat pulsed jerkily. Kent avoided looking at him. The reporter didn't want to see the confirmation of something in the critic's eyes he was telling himself wildly had not happened. For he, too, had thought to hear the thing that had sent the blood from Roberts' face: a low, dim note sounding from Lucchesi's piano. It did not help any to gaze at Loewenbohn and discover that the auditorium owner's face had gone a sickly grey; nor to look from there to the orchestra pit and see that the conductor had dropped his baton and was pressing his fists against the sides of his head while he stared as though in a trance at the piano on the stage. The interlude was ending. On the score a fountain of notes in upward crescendo culminated in a single note, loud and clear, sustained a moment; then a crescendo to the bass. Kent gazed at the keyboard of Lucchesi's piano. He didn't want to look at it; he willed his eyes to turn away. But he couldn't look in any other direction. He stared at it, and he saw the keys ripple in an upward sweep. Up and up. A trick of the light!

He told himself wildly. A trick of the light! In the throbbing silence of the empty auditorium, a piano note sounded loud and clear. The three men stared at each other and then, like sleep-walkers, at Lucchesi's piano. The note faded in the immense stillness … faded and was lost. Lucchesi's widow screamed. She stumbled onto the stage toward the piano. She fell, got up again, went on. She collapsed over the piano, cheek to the sable drape, hands clutching at its funeral folds. 'He's here!' she screamed. 'That note … you all heard. He's here!'

Kent's nails bit into the palms of his hands. Then he caught Roberts' shoulder in a convulsive grip. 'The piano in the pit!' he stuttered. 'It was the piano in the pit! Someone in the orchestra sounded it!' Roberts only wrenched his shoulder free and turned to the woman sobbing over die piano. There was no one near the piano in the pit. 'Here—with us!' cried Lucchesi's widow brokenly.

'He came to our anniversary concert! Carlo … Carlo!' 'I won't be a fool!' Kent heard his own voice sound out, high and flat. 'I won't believe this! I won't!' But no one paid attention. His voice died away. But the ghostly vibration of the clear high note still seemed to stir the air of the empty hall.

Lucchesi's widow stood erect beside the piano, with her arms spread toward the empty piano stool. 'Carlo, you are here! You are! Carlo … tell me … where is the missing score? Where is your last masterpiece?' The silence hurt the ears as she faced the battered, empty stool, as she called to a man a year dead. Loewenbohn's thick lips were moving soundlessly. The musicians in the pit seemed like figures of stone. Roberts and Kent rigidly faced the piano.

'Carlo, tell me,' shrieked Lucchesi's widow. 'Tell me! Please, please, where is the score? Not for me—for you. Your greatest piece … tell me where it is.'

The myriad seats in the auditorium seemed occupied by a vast audience turning ghostly faces toward the stage, uniting with the living folk in wings and pit in staring at the keyboard of Lucchesi's piano. And the keys—the keys! They were rippling in a downward sweep, a downward crescendo toward the bass.

'Carlo!' called Lucchesi's widow. A bass note sounded from Lucchesi's piano. That piano which had no player that mortal eyes could see. A single note, loud and clear … No, not clear!

Loud, it was; but it was cracked, tiny, as if invisible hands were laid on the strings in the closed ebony case. A thick exclamation tore from Roberts' lips. He stared at the orchestra leader, who stared back at him while comprehension dawned in the eyes of both. Then the music critic started running along the strip of stage to the piano. Lucchesi's widow was gazing pitifully, tragically, at the battered piano stool. 'Here!' she faltered. 'He was here. And he would not answer me … would not tell me!'

'But he has answered you,' Roberts said gently. 'He has. With that last note. You heard how it sounded. How stupid for no one of us to think to look there before!' With a trembling hand he took the vase of yellow roses from the top of the concert grand and set it on the floor. He swept the black drape aside and opened the lid—the first time the top had been opened since Lucchesi's death a year ago. There, on the bass strings where Lucchesi had hastily thrust them, were pencilled sheets of music. The priceless score, Lucchesi's missing masterpiece!

11

John Charrington's Wedding

Edith Nesbit

No one ever thought that May Forster would marry John Charrington. But he thought differently and things which John Charrington intended had a queer way of coming to pass. He asked her to marry him before he went up to Oxford. She laughed and refused him. He asked her again next time he came home. Again, she laughed, tossed her dainty blonde head and again refused. A third time he asked her; she said it was becoming a confirmed bad habit and laughed at him more than ever.

John was not the only man who wanted to marry her. She was the belle of our village coterie, and we were all in love with her more or less. It was a sort of fashion, like heliotrope ties or Inverness capes. Therefore, we were as much annoyed as surprised when John Charrington walked into our little local Club—we held it in a loft over the saddler's, I remember—and invited us all to his wedding.

'Your wedding?'

'You don't mean it?'

'Who's the happy pair? When's it to be?'

John Charrington filled his pipe and lighted it before he replied. Then he said:

'I'm sorry to deprive you fellows of your only joke—but Miss Forster and I are to be married in September.'

'You don't mean it?'

'He's got the mitten again, and it's turned his head.'

'No,' I said, rising, 'I see it's true. Lend me a pistol someone—or a first-class fare to the other end of Nowhere. Charrington has bewitched the only pretty girl in our twenty-mile radius. Was it mesmerism, or a love-potion, Jack?'

'Neither, sir, but a gift you'll never have—perseverance—and the best luck a man ever had in this world.'

There was something in his voice that silenced me, and all chaff of the other fellows failed to draw him further.

The queer thing about it was that when we congratulated Miss Forster, she blushed and smiled and dimpled, for all the world as though she were in love with him, and had been in love with him all the time. Upon my word, I think she had. Women are strange creatures.

We were all asked to the wedding. In Brixham, everyone who was anybody knew everybody else who was anyone. My sisters were, I truly believe, more interested in the trousseau than the bride herself, and I was to be the best man. The coming marriage was much canvassed at afternoon tea tables, and at our little Club over the saddler's, and the question was always asked, 'Does she care for him?'

I used to ask that question myself in the early days of their engagement, but after a certain evening in August, I never asked it again. I was coming home from the Club through the churchyard. Our church is on a thyme-grown hill, and the turf about it is so thick and soft that one's footsteps are noiseless.

I made no sound as I vaulted the low lichened wall and threaded my way between the tombstones. It was at the same instant that I heard John Charrington's voice, and saw her. May was sitting on a low flat gravestone, her face turned towards the full splendour of the western sun. Its expression ended, at once and forever, any question of love for him. It was transfigured to a beauty I should not have believed possible, even to that beautiful little face.

John lay at her feet, and it was his voice that broke the stillness of the golden August evening.

'My dear, my dear, I believe I would come back from the dead if you wanted me!'

I coughed at once to indicate my presence and passed on into the shadow fully enlightened.

The wedding was to be early in September. Two days before I had to run up to town on business. The train was late, of course, for we are on the South-Eastern, and as I stood grumbling with my watch in my hand, whom should I see but John Charrington and May Forster. They were walking up and down the unfrequented end of the platform, arm in arm, looking into each other's eyes, careless of the sympathetic interest of the porters.

Of course, I knew better than to hesitate a moment before burying myself in the booking—office, and it was not till the train drew up at the platform, that I obtrusively passed the pair with my Gladstone and took the corner in a first-class smoking carriage. I did this with as good an air of not seeing them as I could assume. I pride myself on my discretion, but if John were travelling alone, I wanted his company. I had it.

'Hello, old man,' came his cheery voice as he swung his bag into my carriage; 'here's luck. I was expecting a dull journey!'

'Where are you off to?' I asked, discretion still bidding me turn my eyes away, though I saw, without looking, that hers were red-rimmed.

'To old Branbridge's,' he answered, shutting the door and leaning out for a last word with his sweetheart.

'Oh, I wish you wouldn't go, John,' she was saying in a low, earnest voice. 'I feel certain something will happen.'

'Do you think I would let anything happen to keep me? The day after tomorrow is our wedding day.'

'Don't go,' she answered, with a pleading intensity which would have sent my Gladstone onto the platform and me after it. But she wasn't speaking to me. John Charrington was made differently. He rarely changed his opinions, never his resolutions.

He only stroked the little ungloved hands that lay on the carriage door.

'I must, May. The old boy's been awfully good to me, and now he's dying I must go and see him, but I shall come home in time for—' the rest of the parting was lost in a whisper and in the rattling lurch of the starting train.

'You're sure to come?' she spoke as the train moved.

'Nothing shall keep me,' he answered; and we steamed out. After he had seen the last of the little figure on the platform he leaned back in his corner and kept silence for a minute.

When he spoke, it was to explain to me that his godfather, whose heir he was, lay dying at Peasmarsh Place, some fifty miles away and had sent for John, and John had felt bound to go.

'I shall be surely back tomorrow,' he said, 'or, if not, the day after, in heaps of time. Thank heaven, one hasn't to get up in the middle of the night to get married nowadays!'

'And suppose Mr Branbridge dies?'

'Alive or dead I mean to be married on Thursday!' John answered, lighting a cigar and unfolding *The Times*.

At Peasmarsh station we said 'goodbye', and he got out, and I saw him ride off; I went on to London, where I stayed the night.

When I got home the next afternoon, a very wet one, by the way, my sister greeted me with, 'Where's Mr Charrington?'

'Goodness knows,' I answered testily. Every man, since Cain, has resented that kind of question.

'I thought you might have heard from him,' she went on, 'as you're to give him away tomorrow.'

'Isn't he back?' I asked, for I had confidently expected to find him at home.

'No, Geoffrey,' my sister Fanny always had a way of jumping to conclusions, especially such conclusions as were least favourable to her fellow creatures. 'He has not returned, and, what is more, you may depend upon it he won't. You mark my words, there'll be no wedding tomorrow.'

My sister Fanny has the power of annoying me which no other human being possesses.

'You mark my words,' I retorted with asperity, 'you had better give up making such a thundering idiot of yourself. There'll be more wedding tomorrow than ever you'll take the first part in.' A prophecy which, by the way, came true.

But though I could snarl confidently to my sister, I did not feel so comfortable when late that night, standing on the doorstep of John's house, I heard that he had not returned. I went home gloomily through the rain. The next morning brought a brilliant blue sky, gold sun and all such softness of air and beauty of clouds to make up a perfect day. I woke with a vague feeling of having gone to bed anxious, and of being rather averse to facing that anxiety in the light of full wakefulness.

But with my shaving water came a note from John which relieved my mind and sent me up to the Forsters with a light heart.

May was in the garden. I saw her blue gown through the hollyhocks as the lodge gates swung behind me. So, I did not go up to the house but turned aside down the turfed path.

'He's written to you too,' she said, without preliminary greeting, when I reached her side.

'Yes, I'm to meet him at the station at three and come straight on to the church.'

Her face looked pale, but there was a brightness in her eyes. A tender quiver about the mouth spoke of renewed happiness.

'Mr Branbridge begged him so to stay another night that he had not the heart to refuse,' she went on. 'He is so kind, but I wish he hadn't stayed.'

I was at the station at half past two. I felt rather annoyed with John. It seemed a sort of slight to the beautiful girl who loved him, that he should come as it were out of breath, and with the dust of travel upon him, to take her hand, which some of us would have given the best years of our lives to take.

But when the three o'clock train glided in and glided out again having brought no passengers to our little station, I was more than annoyed. There was no other train for thirty-five minutes; I calculated that. With much hurry, we might just get to the church in time for the ceremony. But, oh, what a fool to miss that first train! What other man could have done it?

That thirty-five minutes seemed a year, as I wandered around the station reading the advertisements and the timetables and the company's bylaws, and getting more and more angry with John Charrington. This confidence in his own power of getting everything he wanted the minute he wanted it was leading him too far. I hate waiting. Everyone does, but I believe I hate it more than anyone else. The three thirty-five was late, of course.

'Drive to the church!' I said, as someone shut the door. 'Mr Charrington hasn't come by this train.'

I ground my pipe between my teeth and stamped with impatience as I watched the signals. Click. The signal went down. Five minutes later I flung myself into the carriage that I had brought for John.

Anxiety now replaced anger. What had become of the man? Could he have been taken suddenly ill? I had never known him have a day's illness in his life. And even so, he might have telegraphed. Some awful accident must have happened to him. The thought that he had played her false never—no, not for a moment—entered my head. Yes, something terrible had happened to him, and on me lay the task of telling his bride. I almost wished the carriage would upset and break my head so that someone else might tell her, not I, who—but that's nothing to do with this story.

It was five minutes to four as we drew up at the churchyard gate. A double row of eager onlookers lined the path from lychgate to porch. I sprang from the carriage and passed up between them. Our gardener had a good front place near the door. I stopped.

'Are they waiting still, Byles?' I asked, simply to gain time, for of course I knew they were by the waiting crowd's attentive attitude.

'Waiting, sir? No, no, sir. Why, it must be over by now.'

'Over! Then Mr Charrington's come?'

To the minute, sir; must have missed you somehow, and I say, sir,' lowering his voice, 'I never see Mr John the least bit so afore, but my opinion is he's been drinking pretty free. His clothes were all dusty and his face was like a sheet. I tell you I didn't like the looks of him at all, and the folks inside are saying all sorts of things. You'll see, something's gone very wrong with Mr John, and he's tried liquor. He looked like a ghost, and in he went with his eyes straight before him, with never a look or a word for none of us: him that was always such a gentleman!'

I had never heard Byles make so long a speech. The crowd in the churchyard were talking in whispers and getting ready rice and slippers to throw at the bride and bridegroom. The ringers were ready with their hands on the ropes to ring out the merry peal as the bride and bridegroom should come out.

A murmur from the church announced them; out they came. Byles was right. John Charrington did not look himself. There was dust on his coat, his hair was disarranged. He seemed to have been in some row, for there was a black mark above his eyebrow. He was deathly pale. But his pallor was not greater than that of the bride, who might have been carved in ivory—dress, veil, orange blossoms, face and all.

As they passed out the ringers stooped—there were six of them—and then, on the ears expecting the gay wedding peal, came the slow tolling of the passing bell.

A thrill of horror at so foolish a jest from the ringers passed through us all. But the ringers themselves dropped the ropes and fled like rabbits out into the sunlight. The bride shuddered, and grey shadows came about her mouth, but the bridegroom led her down the path where the people stood with the handfuls of rice. But the handfuls were never thrown, and the wedding bells never rang. In vain the ringers were urged to remedy their mistake: they protested with many whispered expletives that they would see themselves further first.

In a hush like the hush in the chamber of death, the bridal pair passed into their carriage and its door slammed behind them.

Then the tongues were loosed. A babel of anger, wonder and conjecture from the guests and the spectators.

'If I'd seen his condition, sir,' said old Forster to me as we drove off, 'I would have stretched him on the floor of the church, sir, by heaven I would, before I'd have let him marry my daughter!'

Then he put his head out of the window.

'Drive like hell,' he cried to the coachman, 'don't spare the horses.'

He was obeyed. We passed the bride's carriage. I forbore to look at it and old Forster turned his head away and swore. We reached home before it.

We stood in the doorway, in the blazing afternoon sun, and in about half a minute we heard wheels crunching the gravel. When the carriage stopped in front of the steps old Forster and I ran down.

'Great heaven, the carriage is empty! And yet——'

I had the door open in a minute, and this is what I saw …

No sign of John Charrington. And of May, his wife, only a huddled heap of white satin lying half on the floor of the carriage and half on the seat.

'I drove straight here, sir,' said the coachman, as the bride's father lifted her out, 'and I'll swear no one got out of the carriage.'

We carried her into the house in her bridal dress and drew back her veil. I saw her face. Shall I ever forget it? White, white and drawn with agony and horror, bearing such a look of terror as I have never seen since except in dreams. And her hair, her radiant blonde hair, I tell you it was white like snow.

As we stood, her father and I, half mad with the horror and mystery of it, a boy came up the avenue—a telegraph boy. They brought the orange envelope to me. I tore it open.

Mr Charrington was thrown from the dogcart on his way to the station at half past one. Killed on the spot!

And he was married to May Forster in our parish church at half past three, in the presence of half the parish.

'I shall be married, dead, or alive!'

What had passed in that carriage on the homeward drive? No one knows—no one will ever know. Oh, May! Oh, my dear!

Before a week was over, they laid her beside her husband in our little churchyard on the thyme-covered hill—the churchyard where they had kept their love trysts.

Thus, was accomplished John Charrington's wedding.

12

The Murderer's Violin

Erckmann-Chatrian

Karl Hafitz had spent six years in mastering counterpoint. He had studied Haydn, Gliick, Mozart, Beethoven and Rossini. He enjoyed capital health and was possessed of ample means which permitted him to indulge his artistic tastes—in a word, he possessed all that goes to make up the grand and beautified in music, except that insignificant but very necessary thing—inspiration!

Every day, fired with a noble ardour, he carried to his worthy instructor, Albertus Kilian, long pieces harmonious enough, but of which every phrase was 'cribbed'. His master, Albertus, seated in his armchair, his feet on the fender, his elbow on a corner of the table, smoking his pipe all the time, set himself to erase, one after the other, the singular discoveries of his pupil. Karl cried with rage, he got very angry and disputed the point. But the old master quietly opened one of his numerous music books, and putting his finger on the passage, said, 'Look there, my boy.' Then Karl bowed his head and despaired of the future. But one fine morning, when he had presented to his master as his own composition a fantasia of Boccherini, varied with Viotti, the good man could no longer remain silent.

'Karl,' he exclaimed, 'do you take me for a fool? Do you think that I cannot detect your larcenies? This is really too bad!' And then perceiving the consternation of his pupil, he added 'Listen! I am willing to believe that your memory is to blame and that you mistake recollection for originality, but you are growing too fat decidedly; you drink too generous a wine, and, above all, too much beer. That is what is shutting up the avenues of your intellect. You must get thinner!'

'Get thinner!' 'Yes, or give up music. You do not lack science, but ideas and it is very simple; if you pass your whole life covering the strings of your violin with a coat of grease, how can they vibrate?' These words penetrated the depths of Hafitz's soul.

'If it is necessary for me to get thin,' exclaimed he, 'I will not shrink from any sacrifice. Since matter oppresses the mind, I will starve myself.' His countenance wore such an expression of heroism at that moment that Albertus was touched; he embraced his pupil and wished him every success.

The very next day Karl Hafitz, knapsack on his back and baton in hand, left the hotel of the Three Pigeons and the brewery sacred to King Gambrinus and set out on his travels. He proceeded towards Switzerland.

Unfortunately, at the end of six weeks, he was much thinner, but inspiration did not come any more readily for that. 'Can anyone be more unhappy than I am?' he said. 'Neither fasting nor good cheer, nor water, wine, or beer can bring me up to the necessary pitch. What have I done to deserve this? While a crowd of ignorant people produce remarkable works, I, with all my science, all my application, all my courage, cannot accomplish anything. Ah! Heaven is not good to me. It is unjust.' Communing thus with himself, he took the road from Briick to Freibourg. The night was coming on. He felt weary and footsore. Just then he perceived by the light of the moon an old ruined inn half-hidden in trees on the opposite side of the way.

The door was off its hinges, the small window panes were broken and the chimney was in ruins. Nettles and briars grew around it in wild luxuriance and the garret window scarcely topped the heather, in which the wind blew hard enough to take the horns off a cow. Karl could also perceive through the mist that a branch of a fir tree waved above the door. 'Well,' he muttered, 'the inn is not prepossessing, it is rather ill-looking indeed, but we must not judge by appearances.' So, without hesitation, he knocked at the door with his stick.

'Who is there? What do you want.' called out a rough voice within. 'Shelter and food,' replied the traveller.

'Ah ha! very good.' The door opened suddenly and Karl found himself confronted by a stout personage with a square visage, grey eyes, his shoulders covered with a great coat loosely thrown over them and carrying an axe in his hand. Behind this individual, a fire was burning on the hearth, which lighted up the entrance to a small room and the wooden staircase. Close to the flame was crouched a pale young girl clad in a miserable brown dress with little white spots on it. She looked towards the door with an affrighted air. Her black eyes had something sad and an indescribably wandering expression in them. Karl took all this in at a glance and instinctively grasped his stick tighter. 'Well, come in,' said the man, 'this is no time to keep people out of doors.' Then Karl, thinking it bad form to appear alarmed, came into the room and sat down by the hearth. 'Give me your knapsack and stick,' said the man.

For the moment the pupil of Albertus trembled to his very marrow, but the knapsack was unbuckled and the stick placed in the corner, and the host was seated quietly before the fire ere he had recovered himself. This circumstance gave him confidence. 'Landlord,' said he, smiling, 'I am greatly in want of my supper.' 'What would you like for supper, sir?' asked the landlord. 'An omelette, some wine and cheese.' 'Ha, ha! you have got an excellent appetite, but our provisions are exhausted.' 'You have no cheese, then?' 'No.' 'No butter, nor bread, nor milk?' 'No.' 'Well, good heavens! what have you got?' 'We can roast some potatoes in the embers.'

Just then Karl caught sight of a whole regiment of hens perched on the staircase in the gloom of all sorts, in all attitudes, some pluming themselves in the most nonchalant manner. 'But,' said Hafitz, pointing at this troop of fowls, 'you must have some eggs surely?' 'We took them all to market this morning.' 'Well, if the worst comes to the worst you can roast a fowl for me.' Scarcely had he spoken when the pale girl, with dishevelled hair, darted to the staircase, crying, 'No one shall touch the fowls! no one shall touch my fowls! Ho, ho, ho! God's creatures must be respected.' Her appearance was so terrible that Hafitz hastened to say, 'No, no, the fowls shall not be touched. Let us have the potatoes. I devote myself to eating potatoes henceforth. From this moment my object in life is determined. I shall remain here three months—six months—any time that may be necessary to make me as thin as a fakir.' He expressed himself with such animation that the host cried out to the girl, 'Genoveva, Genoveva, look!' The Spirit has taken possession of him; just as the other was. The north wind blew more fiercely outside. The fire blazed up on the hearth and puffed great masses of grey smoke up to the ceiling. The hens appeared to dance in the reflection of the flame while the demented girl sang in a shrill voice a wild air and the log of green wood, hissing in the midst of the fire, accompanied her with its plaintive sibilations.

Hafitz began to fancy that he had fallen upon the den of the sorcerer Hecker. He devoured a dozen potatoes and drank a great draught of cold water. Then he felt somewhat calmer; he noticed that the girl had left the chamber and that only the man sat opposite him by the hearth. 'Landlord,' he said, 'show me where I am to sleep.' The host lit a lamp and slowly ascended the worm-eaten staircase; he opened a heavy trapdoor with his grey head and led Karl to a loft beneath the thatch. 'There is your bed,' he said, as he deposited the lamp on the floor; 'sleep well, and above all things beware of fire.' He then descended, and Hafitz was left alone, stooping beneath the low roof in front of a great mattress covered with a sack of feathers. He considered for a few seconds whether it would be prudent to sleep in such a place, for the man's countenance did not appear very prepossessing, particularly as, recalling his cold grey eyes, his blue lips, his wide bony forehead, his yellow hue, he suddenly recalled to mind that on the Golzenberg he had encountered three men hanging in chains, and that one of them bore a striking resemblance to the landlord; that he had also those grave eyes, the bony elbows, and that the great toe of his left foot protruded from his shoe, cracked by the rain. He also recollected that that unhappy man named Melchior had been a musician formerly and that he had been hanged for having murdered the landlord of the Golden Sheep with his pitcher because he had asked him to pay his scanty reckoning.

This poor fellow's music had affected him powerfully in former days. It was fantastic, and the pupil of Albertus had envied the Bohemian; but just now when he recalled the figure on the gibbet, his tatters agitated by the night wind, and the ravens wheeling around him with discordant screams, he trembled violently, and his fears augmented when he discovered, at the farther end of the loft against the wall, a violin decorated with two faded palm-leaves. Then indeed he was anxious to escape, but at that moment he heard the rough voice of the landlord. 'Put out that light, will you.' he cried, 'Go to bed. I told you particularly to be cautious about fire.' These words froze Karl. He threw himself upon the mattress and extinguished the light. Silence fell on the house. Now, notwithstanding his determination not to close his eyes, Hafitz, in consequence of hearing the sighing of the wind, the cries of the night birds, the sound of the mice pattering over the floor, towards one o'clock fell asleep; but he was awakened by a bitter, deep, and most distressing sob. He started up, a cold perspiration standing on his forehead. He looked up and saw crouched up beneath the angle of the roof a man. It was Melchior, the executed criminal. His hair fell down to his emaciated ribs. His chest and neck were naked. One might compare him to the skeleton of an immense grasshopper, so thin was he. A ray of moonlight entering through the narrow window gave him a ghastly blue tint, and all around him hung the long webs of spiders. Hafitz, speechless, with staring eyes and gaping mouth, kept gazing at this weird object, as one might be expected to gaze at Death standing at one's bedside when the last hour has come! Suddenly the skeleton extended its long bony hand and took the violin from the wall, placed it in position against its shoulder, and began to play.

There was in this ghostly music something of the cadence with which the earth falls upon the coffin of a dearly loved friend—something solemn as the thunder of the waterfall echoed afar by the surrounding rocks, majestic as the wild beasts of the autumn tempest in the midst of the sonorous forest trees. Sometimes it was sad—sad as never-ending despair. Then, in the midst of all this, he would strike into a lively measure, persuasive, silvery as the notes of a flock of goldfinches fluttering from twig to twig. These pleasing trills soared up into an ineffable tremolo of careless happiness, only to take flight all at once, frightened away by the waltz, foolish, palpitating, bewildering love, joy, despair—all together singing, weeping, hurrying pell-mell over the quivering strings!

Karl, notwithstanding his extreme terror, extended his arms and exclaimed: 'Oh, great, great artist! Oh, sublime genius! Oh, how I lament your sad fate, to be hanged for having murdered that brute of an innkeeper who did not know a note of music! To wander through the forest by moonlight! Never to live in the world again—and with such talents! O Heaven!' But as he thus cried out he was interrupted by the rough tones of his host. 'Hello up there! Will you be quiet? Are you ill or is the house on fire?' Heavy steps ascended the staircase and a bright light shone through the chinks of the door, which was opened by a thrust of the shoulder, and the landlord appeared. 'Oh!' exclaimed Hafitz, 'What things happen here! First I am awakened by celestial music and entranced by heavenly strains, and then it all vanishes as if it were but a dream.'

The innkeeper's face assumed a thoughtful expression. 'Yes, yes,' he muttered, 'I might have thought as much. Melchior has come to disturb your rest. He will always come. Now we have lost our night's sleep; it is no use to think of rest any more. Come along, friend. Get up and smoke a pipe with me.' Karl waited for no second bidding; he hastily left the room. But when he got downstairs, seeing that it was still a dark night, he buried his head in his hands and remained for a long time plunged in melancholy meditation. The host relighted the fire, and taking up his position in the opposite corner of the hearth, smoked in silence. At length, the grey dawn appeared through the little diamond-shaped panes. Then the cock crew and the hens began to hop down from step to step of the staircase.

'How much do I owe you?' asked Karl, as he buckled on his knapsack and resumed his walking-staff.

'You owe us a prayer at the chapel of St Blaise,' said the man, with a curious emphasis, 'one prayer for the soul of Melchior, who was hanged and another for his fiancee, Genoveva, the poor idiot.'

'Is that all?' 'That is all.'

'Well, then, goodbye—I shall not forget.' And, indeed, the first thing that Karl did on his arrival at Freibourg was to offer up a prayer for the poor man and for the girl he had loved and then he went to the Grape Hotel, spread his sheet of paper upon the table and fortified by a bottle of wine, he wrote at the top of the page '*The Murderer's Violin*', and then on the spot he traced the score of his first original composition.

13

The Monkey's Paw

W.W. Jacobs

Without, the night was cold and wet, but in the small parlour of Laburnum villa the blinds were drawn and the fire burned brightly. Father and son were at chess. The former, who possessed ideas about the game involving radical chances, putting his king into such sharp and unnecessary perils that it even provoked comment from the white-haired old lady knitting placidly by the fire.

'Hark at the wind,' said Mr White, who, having seen a fatal mistake after it was too late, was amiably desirous of preventing his son from seeing it.

'I'm listening,' said the latter grimly surveying the board as he stretched out his hand. 'Check.'

'I should hardly think that he's come tonight,' said his father, with his hand poised over the board.

'Mate,' replied the son.

'That's the worst of living so far out,' balled Mr White with sudden and unlooked-for violence. 'Of all the beastly, slushy, out of the way places to live in, this is the worst. Path's a bog, and the road's a torrent. I don't know what people are thinking about. I suppose because only two houses in the road are left, they think it doesn't matter.'

'Never mind, dear,' said his wife soothingly; 'perhaps you'll win the next one.'

Mr White looked up sharply, just in time to intercept a knowing glance between mother and son. The words died away on his lips, and he hid a guilty grin in his thin grey beard.

'There he is,' said Herbert White as the gate banged too loudly and heavy footsteps came toward the door.

The old man rose with hospitable haste and opening the door, was heard condoling with the new arrival. The new arrival also condoled with himself, so that Mrs White said, 'Tut, tut!' and coughed gently as her husband entered the room followed by a tall, burly man, beady of eye and rubicund of visage.

'Sergeant-Major Morris,' he said, introducing him.

The Sergeant-Major shook hands and taking the proffered seat by the fire, watched contentedly as his host got out whiskey and tumblers and stood a small copper kettle on the fire.

At the third glass, his eyes got brighter and he began to talk, the little family circle regarding with eager interest this visitor from distant parts, as he squared his broad shoulders in the chair and spoke of wild scenes and doughty deeds; of wars and plagues and strange peoples.

'Twenty-one years of it,' said Mr White, nodding at his wife and son. 'When he went away he was a slip of a youth in the warehouse. Now look at him.'

'He doesn't look to have taken much harm.' said Mrs White politely.

'I'd like to go to India myself,' said the old man, 'just to look around a bit, you know.'

'Better where you are,' said the Sergeant-Major, shaking his head. He put down the empty glass and sighing softly, shook it again.

'I should like to see those old temples and fakirs and jugglers,' said the old man. 'What was that that you started telling me the other day about a monkey's paw or something, Morris?'

'Nothing.' said the soldier hastily. 'Leastways, nothing worth hearing.'

'Monkey's paw?' said Mrs White curiously.

'Well, it's just a bit of what you might call magic, perhaps.' said the Sergeant-Major offhandedly.

His three listeners leaned forward eagerly. The visitor absentmindedly put his empty glass to his lips and then set it down again. His host filled it for him again.

'To look at,' said the Sergeant-Major, fumbling in his pocket, 'it's just an ordinary little paw, dried to a mummy.'

He took something out of his pocket and proffered it. Mrs White drew back with a grimace, but her son, taking it, examined it curiously.

'And what is there special about it?' inquired Mr White as he took it from his son, and having examined it, placed it upon the table.

'It had a spell put on it by an old Fakir,' said the Sergeant-Major, 'A very holy man. He wanted to show that fate ruled people's lives, and that those who interfered with it did so to their sorrow. He put a spell on it so that three separate men could each have three wishes from it.'

His manners were so impressive that his hearers were conscious that their light laughter had jarred somewhat.

'Well, why don't you have three, sir?' said Herbert White cleverly.

The soldier regarded him the way that middle age is wont to regard presumptuous youth. 'I have,' he said quietly, and his blotchy face whitened.

'And did you really have the three wishes granted?' asked Mrs White.

'I did,' said the Sergeant-Major, and his glass tapped against his strong teeth.

'And has anybody else wished?' persisted the old lady.

'The first man had his three wishes. Yes,' was the reply. 'I don't know what the first two were, but the third was for death. That's how I got the paw.'

His tones were so grave that a hush fell upon the group.

'If you've had your three wishes it's no good to you now then Morris,' said the old man at last. 'What do you keep it for?'

The soldier shook his head. 'Fancy I suppose,' he said slowly. 'I did have some idea of selling it, but I don't think I will. It has caused me enough mischief already. Besides, people won't buy. They think it's a fairy tale, some of them; and those who do think anything of it want to try it first and pay me afterwards.'

'If you could have another three wishes,' said the old man, eyeing him keenly, 'would you have them?'

'I don't know,' said the other. 'I don't know.'

He took the paw, and dangling it between his forefinger and thumb, suddenly threw it upon the fire.

White, with a slight cry, stooped down and snatched it off.

'Better let it burn,' said the soldier solemnly.

'If you don't want it Morris,' said the other, 'give it to me.'

'I won't.' said his friend doggedly. 'I threw it on the fire. If you keep it, don't blame me for what happens. Pitch it on the fire like a sensible man.'

The other shook his head and examined his possession closely. 'How do you do it?' he inquired.

'Hold it up in your right hand, and wish aloud,' said the Sergeant-Major, 'But I warn you of the consequences.'

'Sounds like the *Arabian Nights*,' said Mrs White, as she rose and began to set the supper. 'Don't you think you might wish for four pairs of hands for me?'

Her husband drew the talisman from his pocket, and all three burst into laughter as the Sergeant Major, with a look of alarm on his face, caught him by the arm.

'If you must wish,' he said gruffly, 'wish for something sensible.'

Mr White dropped it back in his pocket, and placing chairs, motioned his friend to the table. In the business of supper, the talisman was partly forgotten, and afterwards, the three sat listening in an enthralled fashion to a second instalment of the soldier's adventures in India.

'If the tale about the monkey's paw is not more truthful than those he has been telling us,' said Herbert, as the door closed behind their guest, just in time to catch the last train, 'we shan't make much out of it.'

'Did you give anything for it, father?' inquired Mrs White, regarding her husband closely.

'A trifle,' said he, colouring slightly. 'He didn't want it, but I made him take it. And he pressed me again to throw it away.'

'Likely,' said Herbert, with pretended horror. 'Why, we're going to be rich, famous and happy. Wish to be an emperor, father, to begin with; then you can't be henpecked.'

He darted around the table, pursued by the maligned Mrs White armed with an antimacassar.

Mr White took the paw from his pocket and eyed it dubiously. 'I don't know what to wish for, and that's a fact,' he said slowly. 'It seems to me I've got all I want.'

'If you only cleared the house, you'd be quite happy, wouldn't you!' said Herbert, with his hand on his shoulder. 'Well, wish for two hundred pounds, then; that'll just do it.'

His father, smiling shamefacedly at his own credulity, held up the talisman, as his son, with a solemn face, somewhat marred by a wink at his mother, sat down and struck a few impressive chords.

'I wish for two hundred pounds,' said the old man distinctly.

A fine crash from the piano greeted his words, interrupted by a shuddering cry from the old man. His wife and son ran toward him.

'It moved,' he cried, with a glance of disgust at the object as it lay on the floor. 'As I wished, it twisted in my hand like a snake.'

'Well, I don't see the money,' said his son, as he picked it up and placed it on the table, 'and I bet I never shall.'

'It must have been your fancy, father,' said his wife, regarding him anxiously.

He shook his head. 'Never mind, though; there's no harm done, but it gave me a shock all the same.'

They sat down by the fire again while the two men finished their pipes. Outside, the wind was higher than ever, and the old man started nervously at the sound of a door banging upstairs. A silence unusual and depressing settled on all three, which lasted until the old couple rose to retire for the rest of the night.

'I expect you'll find the cash tied up in a big bag in the middle of your bed,' said Herbert, as he bade them goodnight, ' and something horrible squatting on top of your wardrobe watching you as you pocket your ill-gotten gains.'

He sat alone in the darkness, gazing at the dying fire, and seeing faces in it. The last was so horrible and so simian that he gazed at it in amazement. It got so vivid that, with a little uneasy laugh, he felt on the table for a glass containing a little water to throw over it. His hand grasped the monkey's paw, and with a little shiver, he wiped his hand on his coat and went up to bed.

Part II

In the brightness of the wintry sun next morning as it streamed over the breakfast table he laughed at his fears. There was an air of prosaic wholesomeness about the room which it had lacked on the previous night, and the dirty, shrivelled little paw was pitched on the sideboard with a carelessness which betokened no great belief in its virtues.

'I suppose all old soldiers are the same,' said Mrs White. 'The idea of our listening to such nonsense! How could wishes be granted in these days? And if they could, how could two hundred pounds hurt you, father?'

'Might drop on his head from the sky,' said the frivolous Herbert.

'Morris said the things happened so naturally,' said his father, 'that you might if you so wished attribute it to coincidence.'

'Well don't break into the money before I come back,' said Herbert as he rose from the table. 'I'm afraid it'll turn you into a mean, avaricious man, and we shall have to disown you.'

His mother laughed, and following him to the door, watched him down the road; and returning to the breakfast table, was very happy at the expense of her husband's credulity. All of which did not prevent her from scurrying to the door at the postman's knock, nor prevent her from referring somewhat shortly to retired Sergeant-Majors of bibulous habits when she found that the post brought a tailor's bill.

'Herbert will have some more of his funny remarks, I expect when he comes home,' she said as they sat at dinner.

'I dare say,' said Mr White, pouring himself out some beer; 'but for all that, the thing moved in my hand; that I'll swear to.'

'You thought it did,' said the old lady soothingly.

'I say it did,' replied the other. 'There was no thought about it; I had just – What's the matter?'

His wife made no reply. She was watching the mysterious movements of a man outside, who, peering in an undecided fashion at the house, appeared to be trying to make up his mind to enter. In mental connexion with the two hundred pounds, she noticed that the stranger was well dressed, and wore a silk hat of glossy newness. Three times he paused at the gate and then walked on again. The fourth time he stood with his hand upon it, and then with sudden resolution flung it open and walked up the path. Mrs White at the same moment placed her hands behind her, and hurriedly unfastening the strings of her apron, put that useful article of apparel beneath the cushion of her chair.

She brought the stranger, who seemed ill at ease, into the room. He gazed at her furtively and listened in a preoccupied fashion as the old lady apologized for the appearance of the room, and her husband's coat, a garment which he usually reserved for the garden. She then waited as patiently as her sex would permit for him to broach his business, but he was at first strangely silent.

'I was asked to call,' he said at last and stooped and

picked a piece of cotton from his trousers. 'I come from "Maw and Meggins"'.

The old lady started. 'Is anything the matter?' she asked breathlessly. 'Has anything happened to Herbert? What is it? What is it?'

Her husband interposed. 'There there mother,' he said hastily. 'Sit down, and don't jump to conclusions. You've not brought bad news, I'm sure sir,' and eyed the other wistfully.

'I'm sorry ...' began the visitor.

'Is he hurt?' demanded the mother wildly.

The visitor bowed in assent. 'Badly hurt,' he said quietly, 'but he is not in any pain.'

'Oh thank God!' said the old woman, clasping her hands. 'Thank God for that! Thank – '

She broke off as the sinister meaning of the assurance dawned on her and she saw the awful confirmation of her fears in the other's averted face. She caught her breath and turning to her slower-witted husband, laid her trembling hand on his. There was a long silence.

'He was caught in the machinery,' said the visitor at length in a low voice.

'Caught in the machinery,' repeated Mr White, in a dazed fashion, 'yes.'

He sat staring out the window, and taking his

wife's hand between his own, pressed it as he had been wont to do in their old courting days nearly forty years before.

'He was the only one left to us,' he said, turning gently to the visitor. 'It is hard.'

The other coughed, and rising, walked slowly to the window. 'The firm wishes me to convey their sincere sympathy with you in your great loss,' he said, without looking around. 'I beg that you will understand I am only their servant and merely obeying orders.'

There was no reply; the old woman's face was white, her eyes staring, and her breath inaudible; on the husband's face was a look such as his friend the Sergeant might have carried into his first action.

'I was to say that Maw and Meggins disclaim all responsibility,' continued the other. 'They admit no liability at all, but in consideration of your son's services, they wish to present you with a certain sum as compensation.'

Mr White dropped his wife's hand, and rising to his feet, gazed with a look of horror at his visitor. His dry lips shaped the words, 'How much?'

'Two hundred pounds,' was the answer.

Unconscious of his wife's shriek, the old man

smiled faintly, put out his hands like a sightless man, and dropped, a senseless heap, to the floor.

Part III

In the huge new cemetery, some two miles distant, the old people buried their dead and came back to the house steeped in shadows and silence. It was all over so quickly that at first they could hardly realize it, and remained in a state of expectation as though of something else to happen —something else which was to lighten this load, too heavy for old hearts to bear.

But the days passed, and expectations gave way to resignation—the hopeless resignation of the old, sometimes miscalled apathy. Sometimes they hardly exchanged a word, for now, they had nothing to talk about, and their days were long to weariness.

It was about a week after, that the old man, waking suddenly in the night, stretched out his hand and found himself alone. The room was in darkness and the sound of subdued weeping came from the window. He raised himself in bed and listened.

'Come back,' he said tenderly. 'You will be cold.'

'It is colder for my son,' said the old woman, and

wept afresh.

The sounds of her sobs died away in his ears. The bed was warm and his eyes were heavy with sleep. He dozed fitfully and then slept until a sudden wild cry from his wife awoke him with a start.

'THE PAW!' she cried wildly. 'THE MONKEY'S PAW!'

He started up in alarm. 'Where? Where is it? What's the matter?'

She came stumbling across the room toward him. 'I want it,' she said quietly. 'You've not destroyed it?'

'It's in the parlour, on the bracket,' he replied, marvelling. 'Why?'

She cried and laughed together, and bending over, kissed his cheek.

'I only just thought of it,' she said hysterically. 'Why didn't I think of it before? Why didn't you think of it?'

'Think of what?' he questioned.

'The other two wishes,' she replied rapidly. 'We've only had one.'

'Was not that enough?' he demanded fiercely.

'No,' she cried triumphantly; 'We'll have one more. Go down and get it quickly, and wish our boy alive again.'

The man sat in bed and flung the bedclothes from his quaking limbs.'Good God, you are mad!' he cried aghast. 'Get it,' she panted; 'get it quickly, and wish— Oh my boy, my boy!'

Her husband struck a match and lit the candle. 'Get back to bed,' he said unsteadily. 'You don't know what you are saying.'

'We had the first wish granted,' said the old woman, feverishly; 'why not the second?'

'A coincidence,' stammered the old man.

'Go get it and wish,' cried his wife, quivering with excitement.

The old man turned and regarded her, and his voice shook. 'He has been dead ten days, and besides he—I would not tell you else, but—I could only recognise him by his clothing. If he was too terrible for you to see then, how now?'

'Bring him back,' cried the old woman, and dragged him towards the door. 'Do you think I fear the child I have nursed?'

He went down in the darkness and felt his way to the parlour and then to the mantelpiece. The talisman was in its place, and a horrible fear that the unspoken wish might bring his mutilated son before him ere he could escape from the room seized up on him, and he caught his breath as he found that he had lost the direction of the door. His brow cold with sweat, he felt his way around the table and groped along the wall until he found himself in the small passage with the unwholesome thing in his hand.

Even his wife's face seemed changed as he entered the room. It was white and expectant, and to his fears seemed to have an unnatural look upon it. He was afraid of her.

'Wish!' she cried in a strong voice.

'It is foolish and wicked,' he faltered.

'Wish!' repeated his wife.

He raised his hand. 'I wish my son was alive again.'

The talisman fell to the floor, and he regarded it fearfully. Then he sank trembling into a chair as the old woman, with burning eyes, walked to the window and raised the blind.

He sat until he was chilled with the cold, glancing occasionally at the figure of the old woman peering through the window. The candle-end, which had burned below the rim of the china candlestick, was throwing pulsating shadows on the ceiling and walls, until with a flicker larger than the rest, it expired. The old man, with an unspeakable sense of relief at the failure of the talisman, crept back to his bed, and a minute afterwards the old woman came silently and apathetically beside him.

Neither spoke, but lay silently listening to the ticking of the clock. A stair creaked, and a squeaky mouse scurried noisily through the wall. The darkness was oppressive, and after lying for some time screwing up his courage, he took the box of matches, and striking one, went downstairs for a candle.

At the foot of the stairs, the match went out, and he paused to strike another; and at the same moment, a knock came so quiet and stealthy as to be scarcely audible, sounded on the front door.

The matches fell from his hand and spilt in the passage. He stood motionless, his breath suspended until the knock was repeated. Then he turned and fled swiftly back to his room, and closed the door behind him. A third knock sounded through the house.

'What's that?' cried the old woman, starting up.

'A rat,' said the old man in shaking tones. 'A rat. It passed me on the stairs.'

His wife sat up in bed listening. A loud knock resounded through the house.

'It's Herbert!'

She ran to the door, but her husband was before her and catching her by the arm, held her tightly.

'What are you going to do?' he whispered hoarsely.

'It's my boy; it's Herbert!' she cried, struggling

mechanically. 'I forgot it was two miles away. What are you holding me for? Let go. I must open the door.'

'For God's sake don't let it in,' cried the old man, trembling.

'You're afraid of your own son,' she cried struggling. 'Let me go. I'm coming, Herbert; I'm coming.'

There was another knock and another. The old woman with a sudden wrench broke free and ran from the room. Her husband followed to the landing and called after her appealingly as she hurried downstairs. He heard the chain rattle back and the bolt was drawn slowly and stiffly from the socket. Then the old woman's voice strained and panting.

'The bolt,' she cried loudly. 'Come down. I can't reach it.'

But her husband was on his hands and knees groping wildly on the floor in search of the paw. If only he could find it before the thing outside got in. A perfect fusillade of knocks reverberated through the house, and he heard the scraping of a chair as his wife put it down in the passage against the door. He heard the creaking of the bolt as it came slowly back, and at the same moment, he found the monkey's paw, and frantically breathed his third and last wish.

The knocking ceased suddenly, although the echoes

of it were still in the house. He heard the chair drawn back, and the door opened. A cold wind rushed up the staircase, and a long loud wail of disappointment and misery from his wife gave him the courage to run down to her side, and then to the gate beyond. The streetlamp flickering opposite shone on a quiet and deserted road.

www.ingramcontent.com/pod-product-compliance
Lightning Source LLC
Chambersburg PA
CBHW060310310726
48976CB00007B/2276